Five years ago, Luke O'Connor ruined what could've been an amazing night with the woman of his dreams.

There are two things the saddle bronc rider wants more than anything: to win big at an international rodeo and a second chance with Jessa Brody. When he looks at her, he doesn't see the superstar country singer, he sees the woman he's head over spurs for. Even if what she demands from him makes him a little uneasy. The heart wants what it wants…and it wants Jessa.

Ever since Jessa wrote and recorded a rather risqué song about the fantasies she has of Luke O'Connor, she has had it all: fame, fortune and soon she's about to perform at her hometown's world famous Calgary Stampede. When she discovers Luke is staying on her family's ranch, uncertainty sets in. He ran from her once before and she's unsure if she's willing to risk her heart on him again. Jessa has never worn uncertainty well, especially when it comes to passion. She's a woman proud to be in control but the man she craves is as far from confident in his willingness to submit to that control. She tells herself to be patient but with Luke that's impossible.

Is this cowboy finally ready to relinquish not just his heart but his body? Or are they once more going to be bucked by love?

DOMME for Cowboy

JENNA HOWARD

ISBN: 978-1-7751134-5-4

For everyone who's ever given me a kick in the pants
for this dream of mine…thanks.

Chapter One

SHE HAD ALWAYS fascinated him. Lusting over Jessa Brody was easy. Anyone could do it. Getting one's hands on the woman was another thing entirely. Luke O'Connor was surprised to find her at a rodeo, decked out in skin-licking tight denim and an old cowboy hat. No one looked at her and thought country music superstar. When he looked at her, his first impression was not of a multi-platinum recording artist with a couple of awards in her back pocket. Perhaps if he hadn't grown up with her. Perhaps if she wasn't a frequent star in his wildest fantasies.

Feet braced on a gate, she gave the cantankerous black horse loving. The animal almost purred for her. The stallion had just about taken a chunk out of Luke's ass when he had sent him flying ass over teakettle. Now it was getting praised.

"You injured?" She studied him as if she had x-ray vision and was looking for any damage done by that damn horse.

"Bruised. Ego the most."

She looked at him with those chocolate eyes. "The

goal, O'Connor, is to keep that ass of yours *on* the horse."

"Thanks for the tip."

"Come on. I'll buy you a beer." Hopping down, she blew the bronc a kiss then hooked her arm with his, guiding him to the small tent that was the beer gardens. "Got a show down the road. The boys were bugging me so," she waved at a table with her band and crew, "it's this or kill them when they sleep. Hard to find a good banjo player."

She flopped down onto a plastic chair with casual grace. It astounded him that no one was pointing and yelling, "It's Jessa Brody!" Not that she looked like the sexy country siren. Her straw cowboy hat was torn in a few places, her tight white T-shirt was partially hidden by a faded red plaid shirt and her black hair was in two braids framing her face that was make-up free.

"Wow. I'm having beer with Jessa Brody. Can I have your autograph?"

She snorted as she braced her foot on the seat of his chair, between his legs. "Still the wise ass."

Luke patted his heart then caught a harried waitress's gaze. He flashed two fingers at her then studied his surprise companion. It had been a few years since he had seen her and he struggled for words. A part of her was still the kid of his dad's best friend but God almighty she was hot and sexy. "Good tour?"

"They haven't booed me yet. Thanks." She grinned at the waitress as she set down two drafts of whatever was on tap. "I hate to bother you, but do you have fries or anything? He landed on his ass. It needs cushioning if he's going to keep bouncing like that."

He had no idea how she did it but within minutes

there were fries and gravy along with a burger.

"Oh come on!" A man yelled at the other table, standing up and holding out his arms. "Jess, you're breaking my heart."

Jessa saluted him with a fry. "It's a gift. No tears. Man up, Halo." Obviously Jessa knew him, which meant he was probably in her band. She opened up Luke's burger and removed the pickles, popping it into her mouth. "I have a lot of children. Eat, O'Connor. You need padding."

She leaned back in her chair studying him as he took a bite of the burger. It tasted like a burger found in any beer garden, common—like the beer. The only difference was the woman facing him.

She licked mustard off her finger. It shouldn't have been erotic but it was. Her dark eyes rarely moved from his face as she watched him eat.

Suddenly, she uncoiled from her slouched position. A hand curled around the back of his neck and she licked the left corner of his mouth. "Ketchupy."

If arousal had been brushing through his system, it now hit him full force. Before he processed what was going on, her lips were gliding over his and her tongue was licking his.

Holy hell, Jessa was kissing him.

Every fantasy failed in comparison to the rich taste of her. His hand strangled the hamburger and she laughed against his mouth. He focused on her face a few inches from his own.

She plucked the mangled food from his hand and then sucked his middle finger into her mouth. His cock throbbed in time to his heart. Holy hell.

She grinned. "I've been wanting to kiss you since I was sixteen."

"Well," he said as he blinked, dazed. After almost ten years, he was glad she had finally decided to follow through on that want. "Well."

Another finger vanished into her mouth as she sucked and licked beef, bun, mustard and ketchup from him. Each of his fingers was given a Jessa tongue bath, even his palm.

A drop of ketchup and mustard decorated her lower lip and he leaned forward, licking it off. "Mustardy," he said as he caught one of the braids and pulled her in to kiss her. She moved from her chair to his lap as they ate at each other's mouths. Her denim ass filled his hands completely as she settled on his erection, lightly rocking as they kissed.

"Make me come," she whispered against his mouth. "Here, now." Knocking off his hat, her hand fisted in his hair. He stared into the richest brown eyes as his hands rocked her over his throbbing cock that wanted in her.

"God, you're gorgeous," she said, caressing his jaw. Her lips parted as a shivery sigh came from her. "So gorgeous." Her head lowered, her mouth mating with his as she ground that curvy, sexy body over his.

He never would've taken her as vocal as she gasped against his mouth. "Make me come, Luke. Been wet for you since I saw that cocky grin on your face as you prepared for your ride. So gorgeous." A little roll of her hips had that oh-so-intriguingly feminine notch rocking over his aching arousal and he groaned into her mouth. "Like that, baby. Like that." She cupped his cheeks in her hands, her fingers callused from a lifetime of working the family ranch and playing the guitar. She moved over him again and they both moaned as fire licked them.

Gazing up into her eyes, he slid his thumb into one of the loops at her waistband. He tugged up and was rewarded with a shaky gasp from her. She rolled over him, hard gyrations of her hips and he was surprised the chair didn't fall apart beneath them. He wanted to slam her onto the table, peel the jeans off and plunge deep into her pussy. Again he yanked on the loops and her lips quivered as her fingers flexed on his cheeks.

Her mouth covered his and he drank the soft moans as she came with hard jerks over him. Jesus. He nearly came in his jeans as those rhythmic pumps drove her down over his cock. Her tongue drove into his mouth as he longed to drive into her body. His hand slid up her back, under the plaid shirt but over the soft tee. She was flush against him so he felt the fullness of breasts he had been eyeing since he realized tits were great things. Her hand flexed on his cheek and she gazed into his eyes.

"Come for me, Luke," she whispered against his swollen lips.

Arousal shot through his body like an electrical current. From her lips to his cock. He growled and rose up off the chair, thrusting hard into her as he came in his jeans like a beginner. She kissed him as he shook through the orgasm pounding in his trapped cock. Her tongue stroked his mouth to muffle his moans.

"Shh," she whispered in soothing tunes with her whiskey voice, kissing him as she caressed his jaw. Why she was treating him like a volatile bull? Then he realized he was shaking. His cum soaked through his shorts to the denim and as she relaxed on his lap, shushing sounds caressed his mouth. Her mouth nipped along his jaw and he felt the hard exhales against his ear. "I can feel your cum through your jeans. I want to feel it inside of me."

"Jesus," he groaned. "I'm looking for Jessa? Kinda quiet. Reserved. Sings like a songbird."

"You found her." She reclaimed his mouth and he wondered if he had been born to kiss this sex bomb on his lap. Her teeth sank into his lip then she climbed off him like she was swinging off a horse. She drew a fifty from her front pocket and slid it under the basket of fries. "Can you walk?"

"I think so." Maybe. He had legs right? Standing up, he braced his hand on the table.

"Don't forget your hat." She walked out of the tent as if they both hadn't come in front of everyone. He bent down, retrieved his hat and joined her. Jessa slipped her hand into his, entwining their fingers. "Show me your trailer."

He tugged on a braid. "You, Miss Brody, are a witch. Do your parents know where you are?"

She laughed, a light musical sound at odds with her husky voice. "What? Are you going to call my dad and tell him what I'm up to?"

"So Josh...you know your daughter made me pop in my jeans like a beginner? Great conversation starter. He wouldn't want to kill me at all." Luke led her through the rodeo grounds until they reached his pick-up truck and camper. The box camper was pricy but considering the amount of time he spent in it, he decided money wasn't an issue. He opened the door.

"Fancy digs, Mr. O'Connor." Her hand rubbed along the side and she put a foot on the steps, rising up to peer into his home away from home. "Show me. Different than that truck cap our dads had, eh? Cozy back here." She turned and braced her hands on the roof.

"Creature comforts." Complete with a queen size bed he desperately wanted to see her lying naked on. "I do so like them."

She leaned out and kissed him. Catching her, his lips gliding over hers while a leg wrapped around his waist. He staggered back then took a step forward, pinning her against the siding. Her other leg entwined around his waist as he met each bold foray of her tongue with his own. When she sucked on his tongue, his hips drove hard forward and her moan filled his mouth. Grabbing her hat he threw it aside after it bumped his off. How had he gone this long without kissing this mouth? The woman knew how to kiss.

Warm, feminine hands cupped his face once more as she panted against his lips. "Fuck me, Luke." She rubbed her entire body on him and he staggered. It was the erotic pressure of her wrapped around his hips, the sensual feel of her breasts pillowed against him, the wicked way her tongue licked his. He felt off-kilter. "Want to feel you sliding into me, to ride you hard until we both come. Oh God, fuck me." She kissed him again and he looked for the entrance to his trailer.

Luke found the open door and toppled her inside. She hit the floor with a grunt then reached up and grabbed the front of his shirt. A hard yank and he fell on top her, his mouth claiming hers. Her hands battled with his belt while he worked open her fly. He felt like a randy teenager, frantic to get his hands on her, his cock in her.

"Stop." Hands swatted at him and he froze. Fuck. No. She was not stopping this was she?

His panic was short lived because she wasn't bringing them to a halt.

Her hands worked his belt open and her hand rubbed over the damp denim. "God," she whispered as she traced his erection. "I want to see." She scooted back on the floor and rose up on her knees. The front of his jeans were grabbed and she drew him inside the camper.

He pulled away long enough to close the door.

"Turn on the lights, then lie on the floor."

"I have a bed," he said, but he followed the simple directions. Her mouth parted, her kiss-swollen lips glistening as she stroked the damp denim.

Jessa leaned down and licked the wet spot and sucked. His breath strangled in his chest at one of the hottest things he had seen. It was hard to remember simple, necessary body functions while watching her sexy mouth on his cock. If he had magical abilities, he'd dissolve his clothing because then her mouth would be on his flesh. Heaven. Hell was denim and cotton in the damn way. Luke wanted that mouth on him. Now.

"I taste you and horse." She wrenched open his fly and he swore he felt each button pop open. "God, look at you." Her hand slid between his legs, stroking the damp fabric.

"Fuck," he moaned as he lurched beneath the sensation.

His eyes lost focus as she caressed his thigh. Jessa straddled his waist, facing his feet and tugged his boot off. He groaned when she rocked over him. *So close*, he thought as he gazed up at the sensual creature above him. He was so close to being inside her. Each roll of her hips made her body undulate. A body made for sin. He eyed her ass, the graceful line of her back that he desperately wanted to see bare. One braid rested between her shoulder blades.

Jessa Brody was straddling him. Maybe this, he thought dazedly, was how the reverse cowgirl came to be. His other boot was tugged free and he surged up against that notch he wanted to bury himself in. Hands rested on his thighs as she rode him. His gaze was riveted on the back and forth motions of her ass.

"Fuck, Jess!" He grabbed her hips to still her, to deepen the contact. Luke bowed as she ground hard over his cock desperate to be buried in that pussy teasing him. Her laugh was a little wicked as she shifted to his stomach and pushed his jeans off. Kneeling between his legs, her smile was smug.

"Gorgeous," she cooed as she leaned down and licked his cock where it peeped through the gap of his cotton shorts. Her hands flattened on his pelvis and she widened the flap and took him into her mouth.

She met his gaze as she took him deep, sucked hard then drew her mouth up. His balls tightened and pre-cum seeped free. Her tongue circled the head of his cock, teasing the tiny hole. He grunted when her hand wrapped around him

"I could drink you dry," she whispered.

"Holy. Fuck. Me." That talented mouth sucked him so hard her cheeks curved in. He pushed into her hand, seeking to go deeper in her mouth as those dark eyes looked into him. Heaven was her mouth. He wanted to fuck her mouth, lose himself against that stroking tongue. Her head eased up and her lips dragged along his shaft, over the head before releasing him. The air was cool against his damp cock while his body was an inferno.

"You don't get come yet," she said, her face smug at denying him and his achingly hard dick. She crawled up him, a very dangerous feline. Jessa straddled his waist and began to slowly unbutton his faded denim shirt.

When she saw his shoulder, she frowned then leaned down to kiss the bruise. There was a scar close to his armpit from when he and a couple of buddies had decided to ride his dad's bull. Another scar from a tangle with barbed wire was discovered. Each mark was kissed with soft brushes of her lips. She pushed on the fabric of his shirt, sliding it along the floor, then maneuvered it off his hands. He had a delicious view of her breasts down the front of her shirt. The soft globes swayed in the bra as she stripped him. There were way too many layers of clothing hiding her from his gaze, his hands. Time to rectify that.

His hands lowered to her waist and he untucked her shirt. Her nipples were hard, pressing through the layers. When he reached her breasts he became distracted, filling his hands with the lace-covered softness.

Jessa gasped and arched into his touch, her hips lowering once more to his. Denim scraped his flesh. She removed the outer shirt then peeled off her tee as his hands cupped her breasts, the pale pink lace looking nice against all that golden bronze skin. Reaching back, she released the catch of her bra and then there was Jessa.

Only Jessa.

He sat up to see her better. All that copper-tinted skin made his mouth water to taste. She looked exotic and pagan with her full breasts. So much skin to touch. The backs of his fingers caressed down the upper swell of one breast. Soft. Her skin was wickedly soft. The hard, dark gems of her nipples were mesmerizing. She was breath-taking. His gaze drank in the sight of her until he met her eyes.

"God, you're beautiful." Luke thumbed her tight nipples and watched as she arched. Leaning down he licked one dark pink tip then drew it into his mouth. She cried out and it was in perfect pitch.

Jessa reached between their legs and stroked him. He found himself caressing those tempting nipples in time to her rhythm. A little, secret smile curled her mouth as she bent her legs. Rolling her hips up, the denim rasped over his sensitive flesh and left him gasping. Her hand made a soft cave over his cock as denim slid up and down, up and down.

She closed her eyes, arching back while pressing her breasts into his hands. "I can feel you. So hard. My clit is throbbing, cunt aching, all for this glorious cock."

It was hard to resist her words. He had never imagined Jessa talking dirty or fucking him with damp denim. He pinched her plump nipples and she made a low humming sound, so he did it again.

"Harder. Make me feel it in my clit, Luke."

Taking her at her word, he was rewarded with a sharp

cry and a jerk of her hips. His hands slid down over her flat stomach to her rocking hips. "You're all kinds of sin, aren't you, Jessa Mae?"

Dark brown eyes met his gaze. "You have no idea, Lucas Joshua."

His hands slid to the sexy cave his cock was shuttling in and squeezed, his thumbs rubbing the denim over hidden folds he was desperate to see. His thumbs made a softer ride for his cock as he rubbed the seam of her jeans. She brushed his hands aside. "Want to feel this cock. Watch it go." As she stared into his eyes, he swallowed at her words. "I'm going to make you come like you never have in your life."

His eyebrows rose as he caressed up her thighs, hating the denim keeping him from her. He wanted to claw it from her body. "Boasting already?"

Her thumb stroked the vein, up to the head of his cock. Her eyebrow slid up as she grinned. "I'm going to give you the ride of your life." She reached into her front pocket and pulled out the foil square. His lip curled. He hated condoms. He especially hated one getting between him and Jessa.

"One day it will be just you and I. Promise. Until then though..." Her lip twitched, too, as she tore open the packet. Fingers curled around the base of his cock and she slowly drew her hand up to the thick head. Every muscle within him tightened at that grip, at the sensation of the condom settling into place. Her gaze latched onto his dick, which threatened to come at the simple touch. A little smile on her lips said she was enjoying herself. Torture was the way she slowly eased the condom down, fingers teasing and stroking as she stretched it into place. Lightly she caressed back up his sheathed cock and he gave a low rumble of disappointment as her touch vanished.

Reaching up, Jessa removed the elastic band from the end of her braid. She unwound her hair then flipped the waves over her shoulder. Her fingers slipped through the thick pink elastic, flexed it a bit, then stretched it over his cock.

Jessa rolled the stretchy band down his shaft and his thighs tightened. The elastic was pulled wide when she reached the base then eased it behind one of his balls. The pressure was unlike anything he had ever felt as the elastic squeezed him. His hands clenched on her thighs and his leg jerked. She removed the second elastic from her hair. Again this one was rolled over and down his cock, and stretched over his other testicle. Both balls were squeezed and ached. The pleasure was a shocking burn through his system since it should only hurt. not arouse.

"Fuck!" Luke feared he was about to come in that instant despite the coated bands cinched around his nuts.

A foot was set on his chest as she leaned back on her hands. Against his thighs, he felt the heat of her as she sat between his legs.

He was having a heart attack.

"Boot."

His ears were buzzing as his hand cupped the heel of her boot and tugged it free. It fell to the floor when she slid her foot down and over his cock. Her toes glided down to his balls and—fuck. He grunted and she pressed her other foot on his chest. He was sweating by the time he had her boot off. Her legs bent, back arching and up she went in a bendy, sexy move. Yee-haw.

Jessa opened her jeans, her hands resting at the open fly. One finger traced along the parted denim, caressing the bared skin. He watched the slow motion of her finger, mesmerized by that little strip of flesh.

With shaking hands, he reached up to pull her jeans down her body. A tiny pair of panties, with a big ass heart right over her pussy, was all she wore. The fabric was damp with her arousal. Nary a strand of hair was visible. One leg, then the other stepped out of her jeans and she pointed her foot at him and he removed her sock. Then the other.

"Okay?" She eased onto her knees and caressed his face. The touch slithered under his skin and wrapped around his throbbing cock. "Yes or no, Lucas."

"Yes," he rasped out.

"Tell me when it's no. Put your hands behind you, I want to show you something."

Considering he needed to prop his body up, her plan was brilliant. Jessa was stunning. Long and lean with curves where there should be curves. She sat between his parted legs and hooked her legs over his, settling her feet under his arms. As he watched, she stroked down between those luscious breasts and their tight tips and along the smooth skin of her belly. His fingers curled into the floor as his cock felt like it was going to erupt.

Her fingers waggled like a magician and then she peeled aside the pink heart that matched her bra.

"Fuck," he moaned as he stared her bare, glistening

pussy. Her finger stroked through the wetness. She straddled his hips as she slipped her finger into his mouth. He licked away the drop. Her taste was salty sweet as he imagined ambrosia would be. Growling, he felt her wetness on his dick. Bracing her hand behind her and with a low, throaty moan, she impaled herself on his cock.

Luke grabbed her ass and looked at this woman before him. She was glorious. Jessa was exotic and erotic. Her bare pussy stretched around him, her breasts quivering with her hard breaths, eyes glistening with arousal and heat. Never in his wildest fantasies had he envisioned she'd look so beautiful and carnal. Her body gave a hard shudder and her pussy squeezed him, a tight vise over his cock that burned with the need to come but the hair bands prevented it. With a soft sigh, she came.

"Fuck! Off! Off!" he shouted, needing the elastics gone. Too much. This was too much.

Her hand flattened on his chest and she held him down. Slowly she pulled up. His cock was swollen and coated in her cream.

"Shh." Her hand wrapped around his cock as she eased the elastic off and over her wrist. The second elastic snapped onto her wrist. Luke was shaking as she rubbed his chest. He shouted as she once more sank onto him. Every inch of her, he felt every inch. Grabbing her thighs, he needed to hold onto her.

"Now," she breathed and released the base of his cock.

His hips shot up and his orgasm roared through him and his dick. She rode him like he was one of his broncs and he wondered if he'd ever stop coming.

"Shh," she whispered as he slammed back to earth

and the floor of his trailer. He gasped for breath as she lay on him. "Told you," she breathed in his ear.

"What the fuck?" He focused on her face. A tiny smile played over her kiss-swollen lips, a mixture of smug pleasure. Strands of dark hair clung to her cheeks. "Holy shit."

"Don't move." Jessa eased off of him, and disappeared into the small bathroom stall. A damp face cloth was in her hand and she knelt between his legs, stripping the condom away because he hadn't moved, unable to function. She wiped the inside of his thighs, whisper soft over his tender balls. His belly was washed and then gently she wiped his cock. Leaning down, she kissed the limp flesh.

"What the fuck are you learning on the road?" It was hard to imagine the pretty, quiet teenage girl he knew cinching his dick with hair accessories. He didn't want to think who had taught her that, as it made him want to hunt the bastard down and rearrange his features.

Jessa went still and looked up. "Pardon me?" She stood up, looking a bit like he imagined Cleopatra would. "Did you call me a whore?"

He scrubbed his face. His hands were shaking. "No, but you sure as fuck didn't learn that on the ranch."

"So," she reached over and grabbed her T-shirt, "you did call me a whore. Of sorts."

"No." His brain scrambled to keep his mouth from moving. "It's just… You don't learn tricks like that in Bearspaw."

Her hand covered his mouth. "Stop. Talking. Now." Jessa grabbed her jeans and shook them out before slipping into them.

On bare feet she walked over him. She set her foot on his chest and leaned down. "You think carefully about what's coming out of your mouth, O'Connor. You may want to stop talking," she said in time to her foot tapping.

She scooped up her bra. Her finger hooked through a strap and she spun it on her finger. A flick of her wrist, sent it flying at him. The bra landed on his chest, discarded.

"You can keep the bra. A reminder of when you fucked up because you," she sat on him and kissed him slowly, "really liked my tricks." Jessa caressed his jaw then gave a little slap. Anger burned in her dark brown eyes and a flinching hollowness he could only describe as hurt. Shit. Snatching up her socks and boots, she stalked out.

Luke lay on the floor and rubbed his heart. Jesus. God. What the hell had happened? His skin still tingled and damned if his body didn't want more.

"Shit. Shit!" He punched a cabinet. He had been inside Jessa for a total of what? Thirty seconds? And it was the best thirty seconds of his life.

"Fuck." His hands raked through his hair. "Fuck. Well done, O'Connor."

Now she was gone and he had no one to blame but himself.

Chapter Two

Five Years Later...

DOROTHY HAD IT right. There was no place like home.

Jessa had flown into Calgary ahead of her band to visit her family without the boys being underfoot. There were two shows left on this tour before they hibernated to work on the next album. Thankfully, the two shows were here. Well, technically it was only one at the Calgary Stampede. It had been her idea to have a second concert for those participating in the rodeo—something small and intimate, a nod to her father's past.

In a few days before the boys rolled into town. After that it was work, work, work.

Jessa desperately needed play.

After sliding her guitar through the stall gate, she climbed over and hopped down. A snort greeted her and she turned with a smile.

"Hi, baby." She scooped up her guitar and made her way to the corner in case Red Crow threw a tantrum. It was known to happen.

He bumped her with his head and she stopped to reach up to stroke his nose. Crow was her favorite out of all her dad's horses. Once he had terrorized the rodeo circuit as a bronc until he had been retired. Not that anyone had told him he was retired, since he still tossed riders like they were flapjacks, her included.

Back against the boards, Jessa picked the strings while the big, beautiful Mustang gorged himself on feed. Crow was, to use a polite word, ornery. Jessa would describe him as a big ball of mean when he was in a temper. Music, though, seemed to calm that cranky temperament. The discovery had been made early on when Jessa would sing to the horses and cows. As she had taught herself the guitar, playing for Crow had become one of her favorite things to do. He was a captive audience who hadn't cared about wrong chords.

"I'm not entirely sure if that makes you the bravest woman I know, or the dumbest."

Her stomach hitched at the voice and she looked to see Luke O'Connor standing at the gate, elbows hooked over the wood. Jessa never lost the rhythm of the song even though her nipples tightened at the sight of Luke. He made her purr. She longed to rub herself all over him. He was sexy. He was gorgeous. He was nice. Ever since her teenage hormones noticed, she had wanted Luke. Now everything in her sat up with a, "Hel-loooo cowboy" even though it had gone horribly wrong last time.

The song she continued to sing was entirely too appropriate for Luke. *Burn, burn, burn,* she thought as her fingers found the right notes. Her voice faded away and she continued to play as she studied the man perpendicular to her. He was delicious.

His battered black cowboy hat was pushed back so she saw every blessed angle of his face. He hadn't shaved that morning and her fingers itched to caress the dark stubble highlighting his stubborn jaw. Sexy, pale blue eyes watched her with a steadiness that made her body hum.

"Crow loves Cash," she said as she flattened her hands over the strings. Crow snorted as he looked at her, clearly not liking his serenade ending. She reached up to stroke the horse's forehead. "Spoiled baby."

"Baby. Yes. First word I think of when I look at Crow."

Her father had named him Crow for her mother. Red Crow was his official name, her mother's maiden name, but to all who knew him he was Crow. Call him Red and he was liable to kick teeth out.

"Oh, he's a love." Standing up, she walked over to the horse and leaned against him. "Aren't you?" She stroked the horse's back, loving the curve and muscles.

Luke's gaze followed her hand.

That's right, I could be stroking you like this.

Jessa gave the muscular rump a sharp slap and Luke's nostrils flared. Her body hummed. She handed him the guitar then hopped onto the gate. Swinging her legs over, she jumped down.

"See, the secret to Crow is simple." Finally, she faced Luke.

He tried to look casual and unaffected but she didn't believe the act. Luke held himself still—wary yet curious, curious but wary.

"He's all tough and shit until you set the rules. A little knee in the belly as you tighten the cinch. Sure, he'll buck." When she leaned against Luke, his breath sucked in audibly. "But you ride him hard until he knows who holds the reins." She licked along his jaw and cupped the thick bulge beneath the faded denim and squeezed. "Giddy up," she whispered in his ear.

Every inch of his six feet shuddered. There was something potent in making the strong tremble. She took her guitar from him. "You look good, Luke," she called as she walked out of the stable.

Holy hell, her nipples throbbed and her pussy ached. She'd also die before admitting that inside she was bouncing around like a teenage girl yelling, "He's here! He's here!"

Would Luke still buck her control? The thought of dominating him left her with mixed emotions. The arousal was a given. The uncertainty, however, was unexpected. He hadn't been ready. Was he now? She wasn't sure what she'd do if he was unwilling to embrace the submissiveness she had always sensed in him.

Everything within her yearned for him. Heart, soul, she had wanted him for so long. Waited for him just as long. Recovering from that botched encounter with him five years ago had taken time. Walking away had been hard. Staying away from him had been hell.

As a Domme she had learned control. The art of patience. When it came to Luke, however, she had no control, no patience. *Please let him be ready.*

Thank fuck there was a gate holding him up.

Luke stared at the entrance of the barn, the bright prairie sky beyond it a beacon of light compared to darkness inside the barn. Jessa slinked out, a sexy feline in jeans, yellow T-shirt and old cowboy boots. His cock was rock-hard and hated to admit it, but his knees were a little weak. Looking at images of Jessa on her albums, website, the papers and television had a way of lessening the impact of her.

All that dark hair down to her ass made a man want to bury his face in it. Throw in those razor sharp cheekbones she had inherited from her mother, melted dark chocolate eyes, golden skin and a body built for sin, and a guy had no hope around her. He craved her like addicts craved meth. Luke wanted to lick her down then after the rush receded, he wanted another lick.

Rubbing his chin with his shoulder, he felt the imprint of her body against his. Breasts that more than filled his hands had pressed against his chest. So close he swore he felt the gentle thump of her heart. Her husky voice whispering against his skin made him sweat. Those musician hands gripping his swollen cock made him want to beg. The next time he heard giddy up, he feared he was going to orgasm his brains out.

"Dangerous woman," he muttered in the quiet of the barn. He had watched her singing to the cranky horse for a few minutes before he had spoken. The music had enthralled her and her audience. Her voice matched the packaging—no sweet voice, just liquid sex. She had a way of looking deep into a man, seeing his most base fantasies and pulling them forth with her songs. Dangerous woman. "Burn, burn, burn."

Pushing off from the gate, Luke walked to the entrance of the barn. She was cutting across the green grass, heading toward the small bungalow behind the house. Her studio, her father had said with a glow of pride. It was the newest building on the Brody spread, having gone up the previous year.

Curiosity sank its little claws in him to see what was beyond the bright red door. He had prowled around her studio, trying to peer through the tinted windows. Musical notes made of twisted iron were nailed all over the building. The door handle was an iron guitar. Various flowers spilled from what looked like an old claw foot tub. Her mother's touch, he assumed. Jessa didn't seem like the gardening type.

He leaned against the frame and watched her reach the door. One of the many ranch dogs sprinted around the corner of the house. The black lab jumped up and licked Jessa's face. Her laughter made him grin even as his balls tightened. She gripped the dog's scruff and no doubt growled at it before she walked into the house, the dog happily following.

Jessa Brody was back.

Luke stared at the toe of his boot and grunted.

There had been a world of shock in seeing her name as one of the headliners performing at the Stampede. There was also putting a private show for the rodeo participants after the Stampede was over. Like him, she had grown up with a rodeo dad. Josh Brody had retired, though, when Josh had met Fay Red Crow at, of all places, the Calgary Stampede. He had hung up his bull riding glove and settled down to raise one helluva daughter.

Once there had been a few hundred head of cattle chewing up the land. Until a semi had clipped Josh and Fay's truck as he drove his wife back from the reservation where she gave free lessons. They had been damned lucky to survive, though Josh had landed in a wheelchair. He sold off the cows, got rid of most of the pasture land and then he had turned his attention from cattle to horses. Made a decent living at them, too.

Every July, Luke and his trailer humped their way to the Brody spread where he'd spend the month riding Josh's broncs as he prepared for the rodeo. Once Jessa had lit out on her own, blazing up the airwaves, Luke had rarely seen her. There was that one disastrous time that haunted every god damn fantasy, surpassing any moment with any woman. Damn it.

He needed this like he needed a kick to the head. The horse was eyeballing him, looking like he could read Luke's mind. "Yeah, right. Who are you to judge?"

He shoved off the doorframe and made his way to the house. How he was going to handle Jessa being around? Could a man die of sexual frustration? He'd hate to make the books as the first. His name was already in there under world's dumbest dumbass.

Chapter Three

JESSA SAT ON the porch railing as she watched the sun sink behind the Rockies. In all the places she had seen in the world, this was still her favorite view. The front door opened and wheels swished and bumped over the porch. Hands tanned by the sun gripped the railing and her father drew himself up beside her. She rested her head on his shoulder and he rubbed her head.

"Russ and Dena are flying out to take in the 'pede."

"That's nice." Her dad and Russ O'Connor had become best friends on the circuit. It was a friendship that had survived time, distance and a lot of pain. "I suppose he's going to charm concert tickets out of me, hmm?"

"Make him work for them."

She grinned. "I will." The door opened again and she listened to rhythmic steps beat against the wooden boards. Her heart gave a few extra beats. Luke leaned against the railing beside her, his arms resting on the wood. One bare foot slipped through the rails. She listened to them talk about the new bronc her dad had bought from a family that had bit off more they can chew.

"That is one bitchy horse," her dad warned Luke.

Luke rubbed his hands together greedily. "And your point is?'

Turned out, the handsome Paint in the barn, ironically named Prince Charming, bought for the previous owner's daughter, was neither princely nor charming since he tried to launch her to the moon every time she had climbed on him.

Jessa braced her hands on the rail as she listened to the deep timbered voices, her father's a few octave lowers than Luke's. An inch from her hand was Luke's bared forearm. The touchable skin mesmerized her.

"Think you can handle him, kid?" Her dad leaned against one of the posts rising up at the corner of the porch. He looked relaxed, his gray hair reflecting the light from inside. The wrinkles at the corners of his eyes crinkled as if entertained at the thought of Luke handling the rambunctious horse.

"Pretty sure I can keep my ass on him. Yes."

"Good luck, kid."

Never one to deny herself pleasure, Jessa ran her pinky over the tanned skin. She liked the way he stumbled over a sentence, the way the lean muscle snapped taut. Luke was warm, the black hairs silky against her skin. Long, tanned fingers curled loosely over his wrist. Her heart rate kicked up.

It was a casual pose and yet she was unable to look away from the sight of his wrist held captive by his other hand. The grip he had on his wrist made her wonder if he had ever had his wrists caught in black leather cuffs, his arms stretched high over his head so his muscles smoothed out from the pull on his arms. She'd bet her next album that he looked glorious held captive that way. Those masculine wrists needed to be bound, held immobile as she indulged herself in serious Luke torture.

She had known Luke her entire life. When Luke's father, Russ, had still be riding the circuit long after her father had retired, the O'Connors swung by the ranch every July as Russ competed in the Calgary rodeo. The two families would head in to watch him compete then spend the day riding the fairway rides. They'd return to the ranch for a bonfire before the other family left the next day. Now Luke was the one visiting every July before the rodeo. Tradition.

At about fourteen she had noticed Lucas. She had been looking at him ever since. What had started as a fourteen year old's crush had turned into a thirty year old woman's obsession. Her finger bent and she ran her knuckle over him, back and forth. Her father lowered himself to his chair, released the brakes then rolled inside where she heard her mother playing her piano.

Chopin.

Her mother played him when she was happy. Jessa was pretty sure it was his Nocturne B flat Major. They watched the mountains swallow up the sun, neither moving as she lightly caressed his arm.

"I'm sorry about five years ago, Jess," he said in a quiet voice. "I didn't mean you were—"

Her hand clamped hand over his mouth, stopping the apology. "Don't."

Finally, she looked at him. He was, she thought, the most beautiful thing she had ever laid eyes on. His face was in shadows that loved the angle of his cheekbones, the curve of his cheeks, his nose that wasn't as straight as it had once been. His hand covered hers and he slid hers down. She liked the glide of his lips on her palm. A lot.

"I am," he said defiantly. He shifted, straightening as he faced her. Holding her hand, he fiddled with her watchband. "I wasn't implying you were a whore back then. I was surprised."

Surprised was such an understatement, her eyebrows rose. A snort of disbelief escaped. "Surprised? Really?"

He grinned and his blue eyes sparkled mischievously. "Okay, I was fucking shocked. And my brain synapses were misfiring from you. When my brain began to work you were gone."

His thumb brushed her wrist, rubbing her pulse. He looked so honest and earnest as he gazed at her, his thumb doing wicked things to her heart rate and all he did was stroke the same spot.

"I may have been a wee hasty, too," she said. "I'm sorry I bolted."

Luke had terrified her. Not his words, but the way everything within her had surged to life when she had seen him, tasted him, watched him unravel for her. She had flat out panicked, even though she had been lusting over him for years.

The way he freaked out had been as good excuse as any to bolt. It had been obvious what happened had set off red flares within him.

What had truly scared her had been him. The entire "what the fuck," in his eyes. He hadn't known. He hadn't known what was in him and that had scared her. So she fled. Ran like a coward.

Now here they were, five years older, five years smarter and she still wanted to gobble him up, swallow him down so when he stretched in the morning, her body felt it.

Lifting her hand he kissed the heel of her palm.

She leaned down and kissed him, a slow, light brushing of lips. It amazed her at how soft a man's mouth was. Her heart gave a little flutter at the gentle contact. Or maybe it was the man. Then she lifted her hand and licked where he had kissed her. Even in the evening shadows she saw his pupils dilate. She held out her hand and he took it, contemplating the wet spot. He met her gaze as he oh so sweetly kissed the same spot.

His lips parted and his tongue bathed the spot slowly, as if absorbing every drop of the moisture on her skin. Her panties grew damp at the slow swipe of tongue. Well, wetter than she had been when he first came outside.

Jessa straddled the rail, cupped his face and kissed him not so sweetly this time. Nipping his lower lip, she drank his groan before muffling the sound with a sweep of her tongue. He tasted of the yeasty tang of the beer he'd had at dinner. Fingers slid into the short strands of his hair and she pulled on the strands. A needy sound rumbled from him and she feasted on the warm, moist temptation of his mouth.

She poured all her want and need for him into him. His hand eased under her hair to her neck as he leaned in, his tongue meeting hers, dipping into her mouth. Jessa grabbed the front of his shirt as she tried to swing her leg over. She felt his smile as he reached down and pulled her leg over then stepped between her thighs.

Setting her feet on the taut curve of his ass, he tucked his hands under her knees. She rested her forehead against his and gazed into his prairie sky blue eyes. His hands slid down her legs then back to her knees. Her thumbs dipped inside the collar of his shirt, tracing the stiff fabric and the skin below. "Are you coming…?"

He sucked in his breath at her words.

"To my show?" She smiled as she caressed his neck. "Which one?"

Her thumb rubbed along his jaw and a low, purr-like rumble came from him. "Both."

"Do you want me to come?"

She stared into his eyes. "Oh yes," she whispered as her other hand slid over the hard muscles of his chest. They bunched beneath the pale gray button shirt he had pulled on for dinner. "I very much want you to come." A foot rubbed his ass and the muscles of his stomach contracted, tightened. She traced the buckle at his hips. "Do you want to come?"

He held his breath, his fingers squeezing her calves.

"Breathe. Answer." There was a heady rush at having a man at her command, a combination of power and lust that made her blood tingle and her heart race. That it was *this* man made her fingers tremble.

Luke exhaled. "Yes."

His pulse beat rapidly beneath her fingers at his neck and knew what she would find with her other hand. Holy hell, she was wet. The conversation, his words, his presence made her soak her panties.

Maintaining eye contact, her hand finally slid down over the flap of his fly. His nostrils flared and she enjoyed the way his pupils dilated to a thin ribbon of pale blue. Was there anything more intoxicating than physical proof he was excited by what she was doing? A ragged, breathy moan bathed her mouth as she found him hard beneath the denim. She traced the trapped shape of his cock, loving that he was as hard as she was wet. Her thumb brushed over his frantic pulse while her other hand rubbed him.

"It would be my greatest desire to make you come."

His breathing broke and her pussy clenched as a hard shudder moved through him. She kissed him slowly, inhaling those shaking breaths of his, his body still tense as if waiting for the word that send him over the edge of arousal.

"But you're not allowed to. Good night, Luke."

"Jessa," he moaned and she liked that there was sweat dotting his forehead now. Making Luke come on command was fun but this...torturing him was pure delight.

She lowered her feet then slid down, using him as a pole. "Good night." Kissing him again, she wandered inside.

Jessa could've remained on the porch with him. Walking away pulled her in opposing emotional directions. She wanted to stay with him; she wanted to torture him. Because *not* leaving him was the stronger impulse, she had left him, aching and wanting. Denying her pleasure wasn't one of her favorite things to do but Luke was more than pleasure or a sub she topped at a club. That it was Luke made this important.

She never rushed what was important. And she needed him to be sure this time. He needed to be not so freaked out by his sexual submission or her domination. Her heart couldn't handle him pulling away from her again. She wasn't that strong.

Jessa joined her mother at the baby grand bought for her parents' twenty-fifth wedding anniversary. The old upright was in Jessa's studio. She had spotted it immediately when she had gone to see the finished building. It had made her cry even as she sat on the adjustable stool and played *Twinkle, Twinkle Little Star* with one finger. Again, a pitcher with Fay's flowers sat on the piano. In twisted iron, the word *Believe* had been placed above her piano. The word *Dream* was in the studio.

"Teasing the O'Connor boy?"

Jessa licked her mouth and still tasted him. "Would I do that?" She played a few chords that didn't go with Beethoven's *Moonlight Sonata*. She grinned at the thought that Luke was aroused and not allowed to come. Would he last? Or would he walk into the bathroom upstairs and jerk off in the shower? Curiosity nibbled at her.

"You've been eyeing him since you discovered boys had a better use." Fay looked at her, her dark brown eyes knowing.

Jessa seriously hoped her mom wasn't all knowing. Certain things her mother didn't need to know. Ever.

"Be careful, Jess."

"He won't hurt me." It wasn't how he was.

"Be careful," Fay repeated.

Right. As in…you be careful you don't hurt the O'Connor boy, Jessa Mae. "I won't hurt him either," Jessa said. Much. Her head lowered to hide her smile. "I'm going to bed. Night, Mama."

"Night, baby. Good night, Luke."

"Good night, Fay. Jessa."

Jessa turned, resting her cheek on her mother's shoulder to watch him climb the stairs. "Phew," she said as she stood up. She kissed her mother's head and noticed a few more silver strands sneaking into the dark hair.

As she passed her parents' room, she tapped her fingers on the door. "Night, handsome."

"Night, Angel Face."

She climbed the stairs and saw Luke's bedroom door was open. There was one bathroom upstairs and the door was closed. *Well*, she thought as she stared across the hall. *Well*.

Her smile grew as she went into her bedroom. Stripping, she found the nightshirt Robin had put under pillow. Sweet. She slipped it on, then crawled into bed. She wanted to linger on Luke's kiss, on the feel of him coming apart but exhaustion hit her. Midway through her imaginings of what he was doing during his second shower of the night, Jessa fell asleep.

Chapter Four

"ARE YOU COMING along?" Jessa looked at the black lab napping in the shade. Rolling to his feet the dog joined her as she headed toward the barn. The guys were in the corral and she slowed to see they were exercising Crow.

After the accident, her dad's men had built a stage at the corral so he was able to wheel his chair up and see everything unhindered by the fencing. Josh had wept when he saw what they had done after he had been released from the hospital. He still watched his broncs buck and the occasional bull toss a rider without anything blocking his sight. He didn't ride the broncs anymore but he still helped train them. You could take the man out of the rodeo, but not the rodeo out of the man.

The one exercising Crow was Luke, and the horse did his damnedest to remove Luke from his back. Once upon a time, Crow had tossed him. A lot. But both man and rider were older now. On the side of the barn, an old countdown clock ticked down from eight seconds. She watched the numbers decrease. Eight seconds went fast when you were sneezing multiple times. Eight seconds flew by when you dropped hot coffee on your lap. Eight seconds crawled when you were on the back of a horse that was trying to slide your ass up your spine.

"Give him his dignity," she shouted to Ollie, the foreman of the ranch. Like the barn and the house, he had been a fixture with the ranch when her parents bought it. No one had told him to leave, so he had stayed. Ollie was all legs and arms, his suspenders still holding up his battered jeans because the man was a twig and gravity was not going to hold up his pants.

"His dignity deserves a rub in the face," Ollie said as Luke popped free from Crow's back. Crow snorted and glared at Luke, clearly wishing he had horns. "Since he sent the kid flying three times already."

Now *that* sounded like Crow. "I'd hate to think Crow was that slow."

Ollie barked a laugh and she wiggled her fingers at Luke as she continued by.

Opening the gate to the paddock, she let the dog go, enjoying the July sunny day. A young mare got into a game of tag with the dog. She watched them for a minute and wished she were a photographer to capture the moment. A sharp whistle escaped from between her lips. "Egg, let's go." The dog, Egghead, barked as if in goodbye to his friend before racing to her. "Dork."

He panted, clearly happy with his game. She adjusted the small backpack her mother had shoved at her because, as her mother said, "If you're up to your old tricks, sitting out in the hot summer sun without water is stupid."

So now she had a bottle of water, muffins and an apple because old tricks were the best kind.

For whatever reason, her mother thought she was trekking to the Rockies instead of heading to the back-field. She studied the land, the sky, and the distance from the house. When she no longer heard the shouts of the men, she kicked a few rocks away then sat down. She opened up her guitar case and let Egg sniff it. He licked her chin. She gave him a muffin for his kiss, and then dug out her notebook.

Crossing her legs, she removed her favorite guitar—a present from her father for her twenty-fifth birthday. In-layed with black mother of pearl on the guitar's neck was the Brody brand, the outline of a crow with a B in it. A few years later, Griff, her bassist—mentor—greatest pain in her ass, had the brand embossed in the guitar case. Stupid men. Making her cry like that.

Once she had the guitar tuned, she took a sip of water and tried to capture the song that was mocking her. He was an elusive bastard. Teasing her with certain chords, taunting her with a few notes then fucking off. "Feel free to chip in. You think that muffin was free?" The dog low-ered his head and shut his eyes. "Freeloader."

She had no lyrics, only a few phrases that didn't really rev her engine. The song was being a total dick.

Egg stirred, yipped in greeting and she glanced up as Luke appeared. The man looked yummy with his shirt stained with dirt and sweat. A wrapped sandwich was tossed at her as he sprawled down in front of her with one of his own. He unwrapped her sandwich first, then his. A heavy sigh came from him when he lifted the top slice of bread. Luke peeled off the pickles and added it to hers. The man loathed pickles and yet, after knowing him for thirty years, her mother still put pickles on his sandwiches. As if a miracle would happen one day and he'd like them.

He lifted up her sandwich and held it out to her. Her fingers found chords and notes as she leaned forward and took a bite. "Can you pass me the pencil?"

He grinned when he saw her name on the sparkly purple paint of her pencil. She took it and, flipping to a new page, drew the notes. Once her mom had given her composition paper that was still in her closet. Unused. She always felt like she had to write an opus when she saw the tidy black lines. Clamping the pencil between her teeth, she followed where the notes were leading on the guitar.

Luke removed her pencil and fed her more lunch then handed over the pencil when she held out her hand. It was a slow process, but eventually her sandwich dis-appeared. He grabbed her bag, fed Egg another muffin then lay down on his back, drawing his black hat over his face. Egg, nobody's fool despite his name, rested his head on Luke's stomach.

She repeated the tune as she watched him stroke the dog's head, fondling an ear until his hand simply rested on the dog's neck. Man and dog napped.

Bastards.

Standing up to get blood flowing in her ass, she watched two horses race. When she sat down five min-utes later, she sat with Luke at her back, her butt flush to his hip. She liked touching him, even like this. His fingers stroked the small of her back then tucked into the back of her jeans. His breathing never changed. Her heart gave a little quiver to realize he liked touching her, too, even like this.

She picked up the guitar and returned to the song that was once more being an elusive dick. From the beginning she played, making sense of her sloppy songwriting notes. Griff called it a travesty to the music industry. Jessa shorthand, he called it. "I have no song. No, no, no. No lyrics, none, none, none. Fucking hate this song. It's being a God damn dick."

"Pretty. What do you call it?"

"Jessa Brody's number one hit of all time: Bastard Asshole Song."

The crown of his hat didn't muffle his laugh as his fingers slid along the small of her back. Her breath caught at the simple touch. The light exploration sent her heart thumping a little faster. Calluses from a lifetime of hard work teased her softer skin. Anticipation and expectation made everything from her chest to her stomach tighten with awareness of Luke. "Catchy title. Tune's pretty, though." He sat up behind her, his hand caressing her stomach.

Her breath whooshed out and she leaned against him. "Right up until it all goes in the pooper."

"Right up until then. I get really smug when I tell people I was along for the ride when you wrote *Tempt Me.*"

He had been along for the ride, so to speak, more than he knew. It had been her first hit and had raised a lot of eyebrows at its rather risqué nature. It had apparently been too suggestive for a young nineteen year-old to sing. Yeah, had the world known she had written it as she looked at a very hot, twenty-year-old Luke O'Connor while he lay before her, much like he was today, they'd understand why.

The song was about a boy who tempted a girl. Not that she had written anything sweet. Oh no, it was far from sweet.

You tempt me to break the rules, to feel your heartbeat in my hand, your skin under mine.

At the back of her neck she felt his lips, his hand ventured higher to her breast where he traced the bra's underwire against her ribs.

You tempt me to breathe you in, swallow you down, your body deep in me.

His teeth scraped the tendon on her neck. God, she was wet. His breath feathered over her shoulder as his fingers brushed her swollen nipple. She wanted to stop, turn, straddle him and take him deep into her pussy. Her voice got shaky as he teased her nipple, his chest firm and warm against her back. Against her hip, he was hard. Fair, since she was wet, wet, wet.

You tempt me to want your hand touching me as you set me free.

He eased off her hat and pressed his face into her hair, his hand teasing. Luke plucked at her aching and throbbing nipple. Could he feel the frantic thuds of her heart? Did he have any idea what he did to her?

You tempt me to tie you down with my dreams to make you mine.

His hand squeezed her breast, a convulsive tighten-ing as he kissed up her neck, his warm tongue tracing her ear. Her skin tingled from the proximity to him. He was all she had ever really wanted. She leaned against him as he aroused her with his touch.

You tempt me as no one can, as no one will, to stake my claim.

Her head rested against his shoulder as that talented mouth glided along her chin.

You tempt me to breathe you in, swallow you down, your body deep in me.

She turned and took his mouth, needing it on hers. His hand lost her breast, skimming along her back. Her guitar was lowered as he drew her down, covering her with his body. How was she expected to concentrate with the weight of him over her? Her legs bent and parted and she groaned as the bulge of his arousal rested right where she needed him. The skin tingled where his hand rested on her waist her pussy swelled in anticipation. The weight of him was welcome. Desperately she wanted to feel all that strength naked against her, to have him pound into her until neither of them moved anymore.

Her fingers fumbled with the ornate belt buckle at his waist. Once she had made a grown man lick her boots without batting an eye and yet she couldn't get Luke's damn belt to open. She had a plan not to rush him like she had years ago but, oh, God, she wanted to feel him inside her. She needed the sensation with clawing intensity.

Finally the belt sprang open and he shifted to his knees, his weight leaving an imprint on her body as he battled her jeans. His blue eyes seemed to glow and his hands trembled. Need raged through her as she lifted her hips for him to pull her jeans down, bunching them at her feet. The bronze buckle clattered as his broad hands opened his jeans. Her body flashed hot and wet as he eased his erection free. Her fingers brushed over the simple tattoo on his hip. She didn't take him for someone who'd put a lucky horseshoe on his body but the ink was there.

The sight of his long fingers wrapped around the girth of his cock sent her pulse racing. Her pussy clenched as his hand stroked from the black hair surrounding the base to the thicker head. A glistening drop of pre-cum seeped from the slit. *Oh, God, yes*. Pausing, he looked at her.

"Luke," she whispered, not entirely sure how much longer she'd last without him. His lips curled up and he was once more covering her, his mouth hungry on hers. "Pill," she moaned against his lips.

"Clean," he responded.

"Thank God," she said, pulling him close, her mouth claiming his once more.

Against the aching wetness of her pussy, the thick head of his cock probed for entrance. He held himself back, not yet entering her. When her hips lifted, he pulled his back. She *needed* him to fill her. For so long she had waited to have him, to feel him stretching her and feeling him everywhere. No more teasing. Foreplay was no longer necessary. She wanted Luke. She needed Luke. He was the only one who quenched this sensual hunger. The *only* one.

"Finish it," he said as he rubbed his erection against her, his mouth finding her nipple through the shirt.

"You tempt me in a million ways to do the things I want to do." Her legs framed hips and she cried out, arching into his mouth as he buried himself inside her. She moaned at the sensation of all that luscious flesh stretching her. If only she had forgotten the way he filled her. Would she split apart at the first stroke? Her body certainly felt that way.

He was everywhere within her while the summer sun shone down on them. How had she waited so long for this? Idiot. *"You tempt me. Tempt me. Do I tempt you?"*

"Yes," he answered and kissed her. Flattening his hands on the earth, he pushed up with his upper body even as his lower body thrust into hers. Oh God, Luke was finally inside her. She felt full, felt right.

His lashes lowered. *Prairie blue why do you hide from me?* She gasped his name, wanting more. A shaky moan came from him and she caressed his throat then down his shirt to his stomach and around to his back. "Make me come, Luke."

His eyes opened as he growled. He thrust harder, deeper as if he was trying to drive them both into the earth. She grabbed his firm ass to meet those desperate plunges.

"Jess. God, you're beautiful." He leaned down to kiss her roughly.

"Harder." She gripped the back of his neck. He rumbled an animal sound against her lips as he thrust harder. "Harder!" A shudder moved through the powerful, muscular body over her and he began to pound hard. "Oh, God."

"Come, Jess. Want to see you come. Please."

"Luke." Her nails pressed hard against the delicate skin of his neck. A savage growl came from him as he pumped harder. Each plunge of his hips took him deep. She met the driving thrusts eagerly. She wanted him to come. He was so beautiful when he came. The flush on his cheeks, the way his eyes narrowed as if he struggled to focus. She wanted to see him come, feel him erupt.

"Jess. Please. Want to feel you come."

She met the hard, driving surges of his body and she arched up into him, his name spilling from her as she shattered. Groaning, he sank onto her, pinning her to the ground as he rubbed against her, his hard cock desperate for his own release.

"Jess." His face pressed into her neck. "Coming, Jess. Please," he begged, his body coiling above hers. "Let me come. *Jessa*." Hearing him beg for permission made her feel like she had drunk champagne by the boat load—she felt tingly and light headed.

"Yes," she whispered in his ear.

Pushing up, he shouted as he gave one hard slam of his body into hers. He was captivating. She rocked into his jerking hips, greedy to feel him orgasm. Her hand flattened over his ass, holding him against her and she felt each delicious spurt of him as he came.

"Jess," he moaned and she lifted up to kiss him. Little quivers racked him and she lightly stroked his back.

"Don't move," Jessa whispered. Her hand flexed against his cheek. Luke met her gaze as he stilled. "Luke," she whispered, awed at him.

His face was flushed, his eyes glowing from sex and submission. Beautiful. He was so beautiful. Taking her mouth, he lowered her gently to the earth, his hips rolling with hers.

"God, I love that song," he said.

She smiled. "Does this happen every time? If so, you're going to need a private box at my shows."

She explored his back. Her fingers mapped out the valleys separating the muscles then tracked the bumps of his spine. His back was the perfect canvas to be marked by a crop. The tanned skin would bloom bright red in carefully laid out lines. Each twitch of muscle as she lashed him. Oh, how she wanted. Soon, she promised herself. Soon. His lips curled against her neck before he rolled them, shifting her so she lay on him instead of the hard ground. She kissed him again. "Tell me you didn't roll on my hat."

He reached over and dropped her straw cowboy hat on her head so it cast a shadow over his face. "Would I do that?"

Meeting his gaze, she caressed the firm flex of his biceps. "No." His grin was boyish yet bad ass. "I like feeling you inside me." She rolled her hips and he caught the back of her head and kissed her, his tongue deliciously wicked as it stroked over hers.

"I like being inside of you."

She traced the strong line of his jaw, nipped his earlobe. "I also like you begging me for permission to come because that's you submitting to me." He jerked then stilled beneath her. Since all of this had begun five years ago, they had never used words like submission and domination. Time to use them because she was tired of denying what was between them. "You need my permission, don't you?" Her hand slid to rest over his heart pounding hard and fast. "Answer me."

"Jessa," he murmured her name as his hand fisted in her hair.

She caressed up the length of his neck then along the back of his head. His hair was silky between her fingers, and despite the short length, she was still able to capture it. A startled exhale caressed her chin when she pulled his head back so he was unable to hide in her hair. His fingers curled hard in her hips and his cock hardened, responding to the yank of his hair, to her question.

"Answer me. Not with your cock but with your mouth." She wanted the answer. Needed it because she was damned if she was going to fuck up with him again. And that meant neither of them hiding anymore. This was too important. *Luke* was too important. "Look at me and answer."

His lashes lifted to reveal those impossibly blue eyes of his. He met her gaze. His fingers tightened over hers, a sign of the battle raging with him. "Yes." At the soft answer, his grip eased and the small fight won. Apparently he was tired of denying his truths too.

She smiled. "Submitting isn't as scary as you though, hmm?"

"No," he admitted as his hands slid to her back, his arms wrapping around her.

"First time out loud?"

"Yes."

Her free hand traced his features, she wasn't quite willing to let go of the grip she had on his hair. "Your submission is safe with me." Like him.

Oh she was going to do plenty of scary things to him because he was still so new in this world she had brought him into. Deep within her he was thick and hard again, and through his ribs she felt the race of his heart. His lips brushed sweetly over her fingers and she explored the softness of his lower lip, the dampness of his mouth. A low groan came from him as she began to ride him.

"Fuck me, Luke," she said quietly as she removed her hat, setting it above him. "Fuck me hard then beg me for release."

Smiling, he flipped their positions. His mouth claimed hers in a hot kiss that was all tongue and need. Bless his submissive heart, he obeyed perfectly under the summer sun.

Afterward, she lay on him once more, her fingers playing with his. His arms were over his head and he looked beyond sexy with his sleepy eyes. Her thighs were still quivering. Thanks to a lifetime of being on horses and broncs, the man knew how to work his hips. Yeehaw.

"You're beautiful," she said, admiring his face. His lips curled up. "Maybe there needs to be a naked cowboy calendar. You'd be July and look like this. I'd have you clasp your wrists over your head, green grass hugging you. Just like this. Face relaxed from submitting, body glistening with sweat from fucking me."

"You're a dork," he said making her smile. She had never been called a dork before. There was a slight blush on his cheeks. Sweet. "Stop procrastinating. Get back to work, Brody."

"You're not the boss of me, O'Connor." Still, she

eased off him reluctantly and drew up her jeans.

"I know." His eyes shut and a blissful smile curved his lips upward. "No one is."

Again she kissed him before she stretched over him for her shirt that he'd stripped off this time around. Pulling on her top, she wanted to lie on him, inhale the scent of him. That, unfortunately, wouldn't get this fucking song written. After she drew up his jeans so he wasn't tempting and distracting, she sat as she had before, pressed against him. Once more his hand stroked down her back, fingers hooking over the waist of her jeans. She retrieved his hat and laid it gently over his face then leaned forward for her guitar and notebook and returned to her great country opus—Bastard Asshole Song.

It was going so well.

Writing itself.

Jessa snorted as she wrote down a chord, tried it with the stanza before then scribbled the notes out. This new song was a bloody battle and she wasn't winning. Not even by the time Luke woke, zipped his fly, kissed her neck and returned to the house because he had to get back to work, too. He walked away, a loose-hipped swagger that made her want to grip his hips and sink her teeth into his ass. The man was temptation and her body still felt him inside.

Time crawled and she eventually surrendered. "You won this round, you dick," she growled at the notebook as she shoved everything into her bag and packed her guitar case away. "But I'm the bitch who runs this show. We shall meet again."

Jessa headed back to the house, cranky because the

song wasn't going her way. Once in a while, a song was a bitch to write. In the end she'd win and write the lyrics. Until then though, she was allowed to be cranky at the music. "Oh yes we shall."

"Dad once said that Fay Red Crow was the Yoko Ono of the rodeo."

Jessa snorted as she looked up at Luke. "Did he now? I'm so telling." Once again night had wrapped its way over the ranch. Soon she'd get accustomed to the spectacle. Until then she was going to enjoy it on her parent's porch. The view was not topped anywhere on the ranch.

He had changed back into faded jeans and a T-shirt. At supper he had looked clean and tidy with dark rinse jeans and a button shirt. His mother's rules because Jessa remembered the battles when they had been kids. When he had boldly declared he shouldn't have to look nice because Jessa looked like she had crawled out of the barn, Jessa had stuck her nose in the air, gone upstairs, and changed into a dress. He had scowled at her, then fifteen minutes later he had joined them all in the kitchen wearing his good jeans and a dark blue western shirt.

Ha, her first taste of dominating him.

She smiled at the memory and leaned against the post.

"Dude, she broke up the band," Luke declared.

"Did you call me dude?"

Luke grinned and stepped over her, sitting on a step below. He sipped his beer then leaned back, propping his arms on her thighs. Resting her head on the post, she watched her parents. Her father stopped, tugged on her mother's hand until she landed on his lap and then he continued to wheel along the path.

Jessa sniffed in disdain before she said, "He was jealous because Dad had landed a babe first."

"No doubt. Wanna go for a walk?" He tilted his head back and gazed at her. "That way you won't see your dad shove his tongue in your mom's throat."

"Romantic."

"I also won't say they're headed to the barn."

"Big of you." She laughed when he bobbed his eyebrows. "This is new." She caressed the scar above his eyebrow.

"Icy road in Montana. Storm out of nowhere. Winds knocked the trailer around, which knocked the truck around, which knocked me around. Side window."

At the words road and car accident, she felt shaky and nauseous. The memory of the hospital flickered through her brain. Her father forever in a chair. Her family had all but fallen apart until they had put themselves back together.

Luke took her hand and kissed her palm then flattened her hand over his cheek as if he knew inside she was reliving those moments when no one was sure her dad would live.

"Your horse?" she asked because she needed to say anything, distract her brain.

"Freaked out. Pulled over, unhitched and took her out. She was better without the sides being hammered plus if it tipped...Hey. Jessa. Look at me." Luke sat up, turning so they were face to face. His hand to hold hers against his cheek.

Jessa focused on his face. The memories faded as they did. He was okay. He was here in front of her. Alive, healthy.

"It was a bump on the head. Okay?"

She nodded and caressed his jaw. "You're supposed to get your wounds from the rodeo, Luke. More manly."

"Have more scars from life than the ride." He looked at her. "You're so pretty, Jess." He shifted, sinking down a step so his head rested on her thigh.

"From scars to me, eh? Smooth." Her fingers combed through dark hair. A man's hair should not be this silky soft. Granted, it provided her with another excuse to touch him. "Up."

Luke sat up and she shifted, setting her feet on the step he sat on. Leaning back again, he wedged his shoulders under her legs. His hands curled around her ankles as he settled against her.

In the distance a coyote howled.

"Will you come to the parade with me?" He glanced up.

The last time she had been at the parade had been years ago, before she had become famous. Her hands stroked his shoulders. "Sit up."

He did so reluctantly and she squeezed the muscles, enjoying them under her hands. His hands tightened on her ankles, relaxing as she massaged him. Was he ready for what was to come when she was recognized? It wasn't a matter of if but when.

In Bearspaw it was one thing because she was Jessa Brody, Josh Brody's daughter. To the rest of the world she was *Jessa Brody*. Could he handle it or would he bail?

"Yes, I'd love to go to the parade with you." She hoped she wasn't making a mistake.

"Will you stay and watch my first ride?" His head fell forward and a soft groan came from him as she found a knot.

"Yes." She leaned down to kiss the curve at the back of his neck.

"Will you stay and eat cotton candy with me under the fireworks?"

Could she eat the cotton candy off of him? That sounded like a lot more fun. "Yes." She kissed her way up to his jaw then traced the strong line.

"Will you fuck me under the fireworks?" He turned and looked at her, his eyes hidden in shadows. Ballsy.

"Yes," she breathed into his mouth and kissed him lightly. Her hands slid down his chest then back up. Her arms wrapped over his chest and she simply held him, her chin resting on his head. She loved dominating a male, there was no denying that. There was something to be said, however, for the quiet moments. When it was just a girl and a guy.

Not that she had a lot of quiet moments with the men she topped. They weren't looking for that. Neither was she. The men were anonymous and easily forgotten. With Luke, though, she liked that she could push his limits then sit quietly as night wrapped around the farm. It was tender, it was safe. It was, she admitted, Luke. She still felt the sensation of him inside of her. Nothing had prepared her for that.

"Have you always been this touchy-feely?"

"No," she said softly into the night.

When she had been younger she had been afraid of touching what she wanted. Afraid of the desires pumping through her system. Her fantasies had been unexpected—the need to hurt someone. A little pain to see how they'd react. That had made her nervous.

There'd been no understanding back then and she had felt as if something was wrong with her. You were supposed to be gentle and tender with sex and romance, not have these almost volatile needs. She had been terrified of crushing something fragile in her hands because of what she hungered for. All those fears and concerns had come true when she had hurt someone. Physically.

Because she hadn't understood. It's not like there had been a course on how to hurt without *hurting* them. Griff had been the one to rescue her, showing her the way to dominate without causing unwanted pain. He had taught her. With knowledge came trust in herself and then she had learned she *could* touch. Touch for pleasure and touch for pain now meant the same thing.

"What happened?"

Her hand flattened over his chest. "I learned." Beneath her palm his heart beat rhythmically. It was surprisingly soothing, much like the man. "Perhaps I'm making up for all that lost time now." Not far from them, her father wheel out of the barn, his mother still on his lap. Their tryst in the barn over. "Or else I can't keep my hands off you." Luke's lips curled while his thumb brushed her ankle. "Six of one, half a dozen of the other."

He dipped his head and kissed her forearm then relaxed into her, his head pillowed on her breasts. "Josh showed me your house."

She looked north. The acreage she had bought was located behind her parents' ranch when their neighbors lost a pile of money in the recession. Her father had called her first and she had paid market value much to her lawyer's disgust. She would've gotten a deal, he'd said, as they were desperate and there had been a few issues with the foundation.

Community, she thought, stayed even if you didn't. Instead of repairing the roof and the foundation, she had opted to start from scratch so the Philmore house was gone. Her father had couriered the drywall section marked with the heights of Philmores for decades to their former neighbors. The idea had been her mother's. Certain memories, she had said, don't belong in the dump.

"That's quite the hole in the ground, Brody."

"Yeah? I haven't been over there yet." Her parents took the fork toward the house.

"Why not?" Luke sat up as the chair bearing her parents came toward them. Jessa applied pressure against his shoulders to pull him back into place. He didn't budge.

It shouldn't sting, but his lack of movement did. "It will be there tomorrow." Her feet pulled away from him and she felt a jerk of surprise in his body. She backed away from him and stood up.

Funny how she felt flayed open, as if a crop had struck her repeatedly until she was bleeding everywhere. She had grown used to touching him and to have him not let her, hurt. It was too reminiscent of the way he had pulled away five years ago. Rubbing a hand over her chest, she fought to remove the lonely ache.

Why aren't I enough? The thought that trickled through

her annoyed her. She felt whiny and wimpy because she *was* enough. This was Luke, though. There seemed to be no rules for her emotions when it came to him.

She walked inside to distract herself. Sitting at her mother's piano, she rubbed her fingers over the ivory, staring at the keyboard.

"Play for me, baby."

Her mother curled up in her favorite chair and Jessa ran the tips of her fingers up between the ebony keys then down. "What do you want to hear?"

"What do you want to play? Your father is out there looking at Luke like he's measuring him for a casket. What happened?"

"Nothing." *Prairie blue, why do you hide from me?*

Her fingers found the tune of the song she was working on. It sounded sadder on the piano. Luke had pulled away. As if embarrassed or ashamed. Jessa stopped playing and ran her thumb over the edge of the key.

"You look sad, baby."

She was. She was sad and bleeding on the inside because he had pulled away from her. "Excuse me." With her mother looking after her, Jessa escaped to her room. She grabbed her cell and went downstairs and out the back door. The other end of the line rang twice.

"What's wrong?" The voice was sleepy and familiar. Robin Mathers had one of those sweet voices that made a person feel warm on the inside. They'd been best friends since elementary school. When the fame had come, Rob had remained the same. When everything went to shit, Rob remained the same. Her friend was steady and calm and Jessa trusted her unconditionally.

Jessa lowered her phone to stare at the time. Eleven. "I feel raw," she said, sitting on the picnic table. "Wounded and raw."

On the other end of the phone, she heard Robin shift. "Want to come over?"

Jessa nodded and looked up at the stars. "Yes."

"Will you?"

Her friend knew her so well. Robin knew all her secrets as Jess knew hers. Lifelong friends. She was one of the few who knew all about her. It was oddly reassuring. "No. It's late. Sorry I woke you."

"Jess, be careful."

"I won't hurt him." Why did everyone assume she would hurt Luke?

"I don't care about him. *You* be careful. You've always been surprisingly vulnerable when it comes to Luke. Please remember that."

"Good night, Rob."

"Night, Jess."

Jessa hung up and rested her elbows on her knees. A lone coyote sang into the night. "Right there with you," she said, debating Robin's words. Vulnerable. Good word. Was she?

The man emerged out of the shadows, his posture cautious. Luke sat beside her. She didn't look at him. "I fucked up again, didn't I?"

Yes indeed. She was very vulnerable, she thought fiddling with her cell phone. For the first time in a long time, looking at him hurt her heart.

Maybe she would go over to Robin's. At least she knew the rules there. With Luke there was a lot of stumbling around in the dark. She hated being unsure. That uncertain girl had grown up years ago. Yet here she was, hip deep in insecurity once again. "I am no one's dirty secret, Luke."

"Fuck. It's not that." His hands scrubbed his face. "I—" He sighed in frustration. "It's hard to relax when Josh is giving me that 'don't touch my daughter' look when I'm not. So there I am, head resting against the best fucking pillow on the planet and here comes Josh and I have the hard-on from hell, the memory of being inside his daughter replaying through my brain."

He looked at her and she finally faced him. "Did you know he hung the cattle castration bander in the bunk-house? I happen to like my nuts attached to my body, thanks."

"Then you better figure this out, Luke, because I am either touching you or I'm not. I make no concessions for anyone. Not you, not him. I'm not going to hide who I am, Luke. Not anymore." *Prairie blue, why do you hide from me?* "It's all of me or none of me. I'm going to bed." She left him sitting behind her studio and took her wounded soul to the haven of her bedroom.

Jessa nursed her morning coffee as she listened to her parents' flirtatious banter fill the kitchen. She smiled even though she still felt a little raw. It had taken her father a long time to return to the charmer he had been before the accident. He had been angry for a reason and things had been tense when he had been released from the hospital to the point her mother slept upstairs.

Her dad had been the one who had yelled at her

mom about the sleeping arrangements and she had yelled back that when her husband showed up, she'd damn well sleep with him. Josh had grabbed Fay, tossed her over his shoulder, an interesting feat to behold, and wheeled her toward his bedroom. He then told Jessa to get the fuck out of the house.

That night her mother had slept in his room, making it their room.

"What's your day like?" Her mother didn't look up from her baking.

"Think I'll head over to admire my hole. Then I'm—"

A hand curled under her chin. Her head was tilted back and Luke's mouth covered hers in a steamy kiss that made her toes curl. He took her coffee from her.

"Deal with it," he growled at her father and headed outside.

Her dad scowled at his back. Her mother took down a fresh mug and poured Jessa a new cup. Fay's eyebrows arched up and Jessa smiled slowly. She hid it from her father when he turned that dark look on her by sipping her coffee. Inside she was jumping for joy like a teenage girl who had been phoned by the cutest boy in the world.

She finished her original sentence. "Then I'm heading into Calgary with Robin. We're going to go shopping. I have the hankering for new shoes. Did y'all need anything from town?"

Chapter Five

LUKE FOLLOWED THE soft strands of music to the back of the bungalow. He hadn't seen her all day. According to her mother, Jessa and Robin had driven into the city, hence her missing dinner. A few minutes ago she had returned home and headed for her studio.

Now Jessa sat on the picnic table, one leg tucked under her and the other on the bench seat while candles flickered around her, lighting the familiar notebook. A couple of tiki torches burned and the scent of citronella permeated the air in an attempt to keep mosquitoes at bay. The dog that followed her around lay not far from where a fire blazed in the brick-lined pit. Homey, he thought. Breath-taking, he thought as various flames cast interesting shadows over her face. Her purple pencil was clamped between her teeth.

The dog gave him a curious look as Luke sat on the ground, legs bent, and watched Jessa.

At seventeen she had entered the Stampede Youth Talent Showdown and had kicked serious ass. She postponed touring that year as her mother had been adamant that Jessa finish high school first. Then had been

Josh's accident. At nineteen, she had finally followed her dreams out into the big, bad world.

She could sing. She could really sing.

Jessa spat out the pencil and wrote whatever was in her head, then once more returned it to her mouth. With his elbows on his knees and one wrist clasped loosely, Luke watched the process. Once in a while she'd stop playing, her finger doing a little dance in the air as if there was more in her head. Throwing more wood on the fire, he returned to his spot.

She spoke around her pencil. "Beer in the fridge."

"Catchy lyric. My kind of tune."

She smiled as he rolled to his feet and wandered inside the studio. He removed a bottle from the fridge and smiled to see the old guitar above the cupboards.

Jessa had taught herself to play. One summer when his family had swung by between rodeos, she was found sitting in the pasture, a battered, second hand guitar and different books scattered around her while her walkman earphones covered her ears. She ignored the cows around her and they ignored her.

A notebook had been there and curious, he had asked her about it. She had handed it to him and he had flipped through countless pages of lyrics. His curiosity would take him back to the pastures to watch the pretty girl discover her talents. Little did he know that during his watching her in that pasture, she would write one of the hottest songs he'd ever heard.

Twisting off the cap, he returned outside and remembered the last beer he had shared with her. His body tightened and he gave himself a mental shake. He wiped the condensation off on his jeans and straddled the bench. She wore no shoes and denim cut-offs. Luke flicked off a mosquito eyeing her juicy calf and grinned to see she had hot pink toenails with white stars. Tossing the pencil down, she held out her hand.

"Diva." He set her bottle in it and she took a long sip, her dark eyes locking on him. She handed him the bottle. She wiped her hand on his sleeve, smirked then began to play.

He sipped as her fingers plucked and strummed the strings, her left hand shifting gracefully from note to note. Dark hair slid over her shoulder as she played what she had started yesterday in the pasture. It seemed a melancholy tune to him. Pretty, lonely, he thought as she strummed the last chord and let it drift out into the night. Soft as a feather falling, her fingers laid over the strings, silencing it. Her lashes lifted. Something sad flickered through her eyes and he wondered why. Her gaze roamed over his face.

"Jess," he said quietly, wanting to ease whatever was torturing her. "What's wrong?"

In answer, she shook her head while thick dark lashes eased down, hiding her eyes from him. He repeated her name softer, not believing her.

She lay the guitar down and slid from the table to his lap and claimed his mouth with hers. The tasted of beer and the spice that was Jessa met his tongue. One would have thought he'd forget the taste after five years, but no. As a distraction, her mouth was an effective one.

Her tongue caressed along his lower lip then she bit him. A slow, sinking of teeth onto the soft flesh of his lip. The sting made him moan. Something hot and wicked moved through him at the sharp pressure. *More.* He wanted more. He put his hand on her back—the hand holding the cold bottle of beer—and a gasp came from her. She reached back and took the bottle from him, taking a sip as she looked at him.

Hell, as she looked into him.

Her mouth closed over his again and before he processed what she was doing, she was spilling beer into his mouth. Automatically he sealed their mouths when a trickle escaped. He drank her down and flattened his hand on her back, pressing her close so he felt the softness of her breasts pillow against his chest.

A sexy, breathy sound came from her as his hand slid down her back to the crease of her ass and she rocked over him. The kiss ended but her lips remained touching his as her warm breaths bathed him.

Easing away, she traced his mouth with a finger and he sought to say something.

"I was going to try my damnedest to not rush this," she said in a low voice, her finger slipping into his mouth to stroke his tongue, "even though I want to devour you. My plan hasn't gone accordingly at all." She grinned and her smile was half angel, half devil. "But I won't rush you for more in regards to dominating you. You're still so new at this."

Rush! How much longer did he need to wait? It wasn't just the sex. Yes, he had waited for that but this, he knew, wasn't about sex. It was the more. He wanted her to devour him. To stop making him wait. How much longer did he need to wait for her to consume all of him?

A low growl of frustration slipped from him. He wanted the *more*. Needed the *more*.

His lips closed around her finger. She drew it out then slipped it into her mouth with a little sexy purr. His hand clenched on her ass as his cock hardened more before she flowed onto his lap.

"I like feeling you hard as you press against me, your hand gripping me." Her damp finger painted his mouth with the moisture from her mouth. "I told myself I wouldn't rush this when all I want to do is see how long until you're begging me to fuck you."

Words strangled in his chest, tangled around the sudden increase in his heart rate. His hand tightened even more as he pressed her closer.

"You have no idea, Luke. No idea." She kissed him again and his other hand flattened on her back in an attempt to get her closer and to change her mind. Her hand gripped the back of his shirt and that was hot. As if she needed to contain herself.

"Then give me an idea." His voice was raspy, as if he hadn't talked in a year, but she smelled good, she felt good, she tasted good. And he wanted more.

She cupped his jaw and turned his head so her lips brushed his ear. "By begging I don't mean, 'Please fuck me, Jess. Please let me come, Jess.' I mean I want your body covered in sweat, your cock on fire because I won't let you come. I want every muscle in your body tense and straining with need. I want you *begging* me, Luke. Begging for release, begging for more. Begging me to take you, to ease the fire raging in your body that I stoked for hours."

Her thumb pressed behind his jaw bone, tilting his head back. "I want this gorgeous body held in place by rope and my will. Only when I take that big, beautiful cock of yours into me will I open the chute and let you loose as you buck beneath me, a beautiful stallion whose one fate in this world is to break to my saddle.

"I want you covered in marks because I took a crop or whip to you because the image of you straining against the pain makes me wet. I want you on your knees, body pliant and submissive to me. *Only* me." Suddenly she released his jaw.

He was panting, achingly hard and gripping the back of her shirt. His body was tight and hard, his cock throbbing against the denim keeping him from her. Remembering the feel of her hot, wet pussy clinging to him, remembering the way she cried out his name, remembering Jessa.

"That is my idea," she whispered. "Now." Her hand caressed down his neck before she whispered, "Come."

It was like before, like every time. An electrical current shot from her mouth to his cock. He shuddered as the orgasm hit him, confined once again by his damn jeans. If it had been unsatisfying to come in his jeans before, now he loathed it since he been inside her. A strangled sound came from him as he drove hard against her core. His head fell to her shoulder as he panted hard, much like her stallion fighting the bit, the saddle. The control no longer his.

She lightly caressed the back of his neck. "I love the way you come," she whispered in his ear, her siren voice shivering down his spine and vibrating into his dick. "The way you come for me. The way you come in me. You're so indescribably gorgeous."

Fuck. He turned his head, settling between her breasts. He felt limp. Drained. She laid her cheek on his head, stroking his back. A log on the fire popped. Her nipple was swollen through the fabric and he heard the muffled thuds of her heart beating. The scent of the wood smoke and prairies drifted from her.

He hadn't fully comprehended what she stirred in him until that day at the rodeo five years ago. The blinders had fallen from his eyes in that one earth-shattering moment. She had been bossing him around all their lives but that day had changed it all.

A hunger had clawed through him and indescribable needs had bubbled to the surface.

After he had fucked it up and she had disappeared, he had been left to stumble blindly around in the light. Navigating on his own had sucked. He had wanted her there. Needed her there. He had contemplated other Dommes but everything in his soul had called out for this woman. This sexy, dominant female who made him hard, made him ache, made him feel right on the inside.

Everything she had just said to him was what burned inside of him too. He wanted too. He wanted all of that with her. *Only* her.

Jessa Brody. His Jessa—Mistress of his heart.

Wood popped in the fire, sending sparks into the night. "Take a shower," she said softly as she kissed his forehead. His hands fell to his thighs as she eased off his lap. "It's not much but it will get the job done." She picked up his beer and dumped it over the fire. His hands were braced on the bench and he stared at the grains of wood. He felt…numb, yet vibrantly alive.

"Hey." Fingers slid into his hair, fisting and she tugged his head back. "Shower."

After searching his face, she leaned down to kiss him, a slow lingering kiss he felt in his toes. "Come on." She took his hand and began to walk. His choice was to follow or be dragged off the bench. He already felt as if he had hit the floor.

Jessa led him through the studio's kitchen into a small bathroom. She pushed him so he was leaning against the pedestal sink. Kneeling down, she tapped his knee. Bracing himself, he lifted his foot and watched her pry off his boot, then the other one. She ran her hands up his legs and stopped at his thighs.

A little smile curled her lips as she studied his jeans then she was opening his belt. Her thumb rubbed over the buckle. "That was a good ride."

He jerked and saw she was looking at his buckle and not his groin. The rodeo was a few hours from his ranch. Every year he participated, had since he had been a kid and his dad had plopped him on top of a sheep in the sheep riding. Two years ago, he had earned the buckle not from winning the ride but more of a "lifetime achievement" award. Or as his dad had put it, a lifetime ass bouncing award. "You saw?"

"Yes." She opened his fly and tugged his jeans and boxers down.

"I didn't see you."

"No."

He frowned. "Why the fuck not?"

"I was mad."

"At me?" God damn it, she hadn't spoken to him then. Two years ago they had been in the same air space and nothing? What the hell?

Shaking her head, she drew off his socks. "Something else. I was not in a good headspace for you. I'd have hurt you. And not in a good way."

He studied her face. "What happened?" She shook her head again as she knelt at his feet. "Jess."

"It's forgotten now. Don't gnaw on it, Luke. Had I followed through on my thoughts…" She shut her eyes at whatever she saw in her mind. "You have great legs." She rubbed her cheek on his thigh as she caressed the backs of his legs. "Mama calls them bucker's thighs—rock hard from squeezing big, strong animals. Dad would get this smirk and I decided I wanted to know nothing more."

Hell, he was getting hard again. How the hell did she do this to him?

She stood and began to unbutton his shirt from the neck down. By the time she reached the last two buttons he was erect, rising towards her like she was the sun. The sleeves were unrolled to his wrists. "You're hard all over, aren't you, Luke?"

A black eyebrow arched as she looked at him. Her hands caressed up his arms then she eased his shirt over his shoulders. "Apparently," he drawled.

"Gorgeous." She gazed at him from head to toe. "Shower." She rose on her toes and kissed him. "I want to imagine you jerking off in my shower as you relive and realize." His cock lightly was caressed lightly before she walked out of the bathroom.

"Realize what?"

Fingers waved at him as she disappeared from sight. He growled in frustration and rubbed his face. She was the most frustrating woman on so many levels. With a sigh, he pushed off of the sink and reached in to the shower stall and turned on the water. He stepped in and closed the tinted glass. Shutting his eyes, he leaned against the wall as water beat against his aroused body. She tied him up in knots. Had for years.

I want this gorgeous body held in place by rope and my will. Only when I take that big, beautiful cock of yours into my body will I open the chute and let you loose as you buck beneath me, a beautiful stallion whose one fate in this world is to break to my saddle.

Held in place by rope and my will.

Desire pounded fresh in his cock and he lurched forward, turning the water to cold. God, that siren voice in his ear as she barely touched him. She made him want. She always had. Almost half his life had been spent wanting her, craving her. Bracing a hand on the wall, he stared at the drain and rushing water.

His first true sexual fantasy had been about her. He had been sixteen, not eager to travel with his folks. He wanted to be with his friends, flirt with the girls. They had pulled up at the Brody spread and he had been in a piss-ass, pissy mood to the point he thought his mom was going to hog-tie him to the back bumper when they reached the Canada-US border.

It had been maybe two or three years since they had stopped by. It had been a few months before the accident when the world was innocent. Jessa had…she had damn near stopped his heart. At sixteen, discovering there were powers to being a female, she had flirted with all the men. Even his dad, to his horror.

He had wanted to kiss her. Kiss that sassy mouth that had the ability to sing down the moon. He had planned it, to the minute, on the moves he was going to take. She had been in the tack room, holding a spur. That god damn spur.

Her fingers had flicked it, pondering it then as he watched she had rolled it across her breasts, tracing the line of her red tube top. And holy fuck. Her lips had curled a bit and fire had licked through him until he had been afraid he was going to come in his jeans. She spotted him and took his hand. Lightly, she ran the spur up from his wrist to his elbow, that little Jessa smile playing upon her lips.

"Nice, eh?" Those dark eyes had looked into him, far into him as he felt every press of metal on his flesh, the heat of her hand on his wrist.

He had shrugged and said it was only metal, left her in the barn and damn near killed himself as he jerked off to the sight of that smile, that spur, his flesh, her flesh. He had fucking erupted on a hay bale he had stopped behind. Years later he still felt that god damn spur press against his flesh. *Nice, eh?*

By ropes and my will.

And look at you now, O'Connor, standing under cold water, cock in his hand, that same God damn smile against his ear. *Now, come.*

He almost felt those ropes on his wrists. He saw that

pink heart on her panties from five years ago peeling aside to show him the sweetest pussy on the god damn planet. She slowly took his throbbing cock into her and he immediately came. *Now, come.*

That lean, lush body claiming him. God, that had been the best sex of his life—thirty seconds inside Jessa Brody. That hand cupping his cock in the barn as she told him how to make Crow behave.

Now, come.

Her sultry whisper, always. *Always.*

"God," he groaned as his entire body jerked and he finally came. "Jess." His cum vanished down the drain and he braced both hands on the wall. Without arousal clawing at him, he noticed the cold water and he adjusted it to warm. Water pounded over muscles that were still tense because, fuck, jerking off to memories of Jessa was tiring and unsatisfying. God, he wanted her. He wanted more.

"God, yes." He leaned against the wall again and let his head fall against the tile.

When the water turned completely cold, he turned it off. A towel hung on the door and he didn't know if it had been there before, all his attention had been focused on Jessa. What he knew hadn't been there before was his gray track pants folded on the toilet seat along with sneakers. His clothes were gone. As he dried off he looked at the mirror. He froze.

Lips in bright red were on the glass along with *Come. Now.*

"Bitch," he muttered as he pulled on his pants. He scrubbed off the lipstick with his towel, turned off the lights and wandered into the darkened kitchen. A candle glowed on the counter and a key was taped above the bolt lock. After blowing out the candle, he took the key, locked the door to her studio and walked by the table where she had unraveled him.

The light above the back door glowed and with a sigh he jogged toward it. He tucked the key into his pocket as he entered the main house. He needed no lights to get to the room he used when he stayed here but one was glowing. A candle flickered by his bed, probably lit by Jessa. Exhausted, he toed off his sneakers, stripped off the pants and crawled into bed. He lay there, staring at the ceiling as his brain continued to throw images at him.

It was going to be a long night.

Chapter Six

WAS THERE ANYTHING more satisfying than a man snarly because he was sexually frustrated?

As she sat on the wooden swing by the back door, Jessa thought not.

There was a lot of cursing coming from the corral. Her mother stepped onto the back porch to see what was setting Luke off. Fay looked over at Jessa, who pulled an innocent expression.

"Ha. As if I believe that look." Sitting down beside Jessa, her mother picked up her notebook to scan the phrases she had scribbled. The word Prairie Blue was circled at the top followed by a question mark. "Is this going to be another one of those songs where there's a lecture at church on how our children are being led astray?"

Jessa laughed. She liked that. "Yes."

"Mrs. Chezki told me your song *Tempt Me* was disgusting, but do you think you would sign her album for her?" Her mom smoothed a hand down Jessa's hair and leaned over and kissed her cheek. "I used to worry about you. When that song came out, it was frighteningly sexual for a girl your age. Intense. I was positive I was going to become a grandmother way too early even though the only boy I remember you looking at was Luke. I worried about what kind of trouble you two got into out there." Fay waved her hand out to the pasture.

Luke exited the fenced area and slapped his hand against his thigh. One of the guys tossed him a bottled water from the cooler and he twisted off the cap and drained the water. Jess said, "The one time we had sex—"

Her mother cleared her throat, clearly not comfortable hearing about her daughter's sexcapades. Fair enough. Damned if she was going to share them.

"I was twenty-five."

The look of relief on her mother's face was almost laughable. "Oh."

They both watched as Luke took a second bottle, leaned forward and dumped the water over his head. Mmm, wet Luke. It was a great view even from a distance. The water would soak through his shirt to his skin, drops clinging to his lashes. If he was close, she'd catch any drips off his mouth with her tongue.

"Oh," her mother repeated softly. "Why? I mean, not that I'm not relieved my teenage daughter wasn't rolling around the pasture all those summers... But that's a long wait."

Shit. Jessa did not want to have this conversation with her mom. "Yes. And I'm not willing to share the why with you."

"Does he know?"

Jessa rested her arm on the side of her guitar as Luke pushed his wet hair out of his face. His hand wiped on his jeans while he looked her way. "Most of it."

"For the sake of his sanity, don't make him wait five more years." Her mom squeezed Jessa's thigh then wandered back inside.

Her thumb caressed over the strings as Luke returned to the corral. She stood up, set her guitar down on the bench and wandered over to see what had him cursing. Aside from her.

Luke worked with the new horse, Prince Charming. He spoke to the horse in a low, gentle voice. "I know. That saddle's like a tuxedo. Or a tie. Horrific things. But you keep that up and I can't get it off. Then where will you be? Forever. Trapped in a suit." Luke shuddered and stroked the horse's neck, calming him.

She climbed onto the fence, her feet resting on a lower plank and her arms draped over the upper one. The horse stilled and gave Luke a tragic look.

"I know. Who wants to wear that shit?"

She smiled. He was so…calm. Steady. He kept up the suit trash talk as he released the cinch and pulled off the saddle. Ollie walked toward him, the rigging used for bare bronc riding hooked over his shoulder. They swapped and Luke settled the rigging behind the horse's shoulder. The horse gave Luke a suspicious look, like he was getting another saddle.

"Dude, would I do that to you?" Luke cinched it in place then adjusted the handhold. "Now look at you, tricked out like a bad-assed mother bucker."

Jessa chuckled as Luke stepped back and folded his arms over his chest. He nodded. "Yeah, you're a bad-ass mother bucker, aren't you?" He caressed down the horse's back. "Let's see what's in your back pocket."

His hand stroked over the tawny flank and the horse came to life. Luke ducked and spun away with practice as the horse twisted in the air in a lithe, powerful motion. His hindquarters snapped up as if he was going to kick the moon.

"That's showing off. How about you and I have some bad-assed fun?" He sounded eager to get onto the horse, to see what Prince would do.

Ollie came and held the horse, stroking it and murmuring softly to him in German. Ollie gave Luke a leg up onto the horse's back and he gripped the rigging handhold. Two pick up men were on horses in the corral. They were there to pluck him off Prince should he not get thrown. Around her, men were wagering on how soon Luke would get tossed. It wasn't a matter of if but when with Prince.

There was five seconds of horrified, betrayed shock from the horse. Luke's fingers flexed out one by one, then curving around the handhold. Then the bad-assed mother bucker erupted. It was volatile, it was grace. It was animal, it was man.

There was nothing like seeing Luke do what he was born to do. The horse twisted left and right in the air, kicking, dipping his head as he did his damnedest to remove the pain in the ass on his back. Luke flowed left, right, back, forward as he did his damnedest to remain on the horse. Arousal began to hum through her as she watched him. He was catapulted two feet up from the horse and hit the ground hard, but rolled to his feet.

"Now *that*," he crowed, "is a bad-assed, mother bucking ride."

Luke brushed the dirt from his ass then picked up his hat, knocking the dirt from it. Rid of his pain in the ass, the horse settled down.

"Three point five seconds, O'Connor," her dad called out.

"Yeah but it was a great three point five seconds." He shook out his leg and rubbed the horse's neck. "Wanna go again?"

More than once he climbed onto Prince's back. More than once he was dumped on the ground. Both man and horse seemed to be having fun. Crazy creatures. Her father was keeping the name. Josh loved the sense of irony.

Luke was getting the rhythm. He was beautiful as he stretched out backward when Charming thrust his hind legs up. The man and horse battling for control would be an image that would stay with her forever. The sheer determination on his face, the athletic beauty of his body.

There was disappointment when Charming suddenly twisted left then right while kicking because Luke hit the ground. The man was on a mission. It was beyond sexy to watch him ride. Concentration was etched into the way his eyebrows were lowered over his eyes. The determination on his face was intense. She knew what it was like to have him focused like that on her.

Sexy. So sexy.

Her body was humming. He swept up the hat he had lost and brushed it off as he glanced her way.

"Six one. Record on him," her father called out from his position on the raised platform.

"I'll hit eight," Luke vowed as he stared at her. The battered, black cowboy hat was settled on his head and he tipped the front down. A simple gesture. A howdy-do that made her pussy spasm with need. She wanted him. Bad. Now. Here. She wiggled two fingers and he walked toward her. Covered in dirt and sweat, his eyes glowed from the ride, the thrill, the joy of it all.

Luke set his boot on the board between hers and pulled himself up so they were almost eye to eye. She kissed him because he was glorious. His mouth fed at hers, his tongue meeting hers. Hunger from all the teasing spilled out between their mouths.

"I am so wet for you, Luke," she whispered huskily into his mouth. A shudder jerked through his body and he all but fell, his foot sliding off the step. He gazed up at her and she stood up.

"So wet," she murmured, "that I'm going to go masturbate to the memory of that ride."

Luke sucked in his breath, his cheeks hollowing. He gripped the wall between them.

"I'm going to cum," she leaned down, "screaming your name as I imagine you moving like that beneath me. Athletic grace, primal beauty, muscles straining and contracting with the primary goal to get me off. So wet." Turning, she walked away.

"And Luke?" She looked at him over her shoulder. "It will be so good."

She added an extra sway to her hips. Distantly she heard Ollie asking her dad if he still kept his shotgun lying around. She fanned herself with the notebook, her heart thudding hard.

She wanted him. Oh how she wanted him. Jessa wanted to know his limits. How far could she push him before he tossed her off the ride? Time to find out. Because he would buck. He had from the beginning.

After making sure her parents were fast asleep, Jessa eased from her bed. She wasn't entirely sure what she was going to do, but she wasn't going to be the only one not sleeping.

Tiptoeing across the hall, she paused and rolled her eyes. Tiptoeing? Really? Shaking her head, she opened the door to his room and slipped in.

The man was neat, which made for a pleasant surprise because tripping would've killed her sneaking. Nothing said sexy like going "oof" in the dark and crashing into something.

Turning on the bedside lamp, Jessa sat on the side of the bed. She had traveled the world, mingled with the beautiful people, and he was still the most irresistable creature she had seen. She liked how he slept. An arm over his head, hand relaxed and his pinky finger curled over the pine bars. That one finger was deliciously hot.

His soft, sexy mouth was parted. It was sweet while the dark stubble on his jaw was sexy. He was lean and ripped with muscles. Her hand tingled to stroke that smooth skin, trace the dips separating his muscles. The sheet slid low on one hip, the bone bared like temptation. His other hand was under his ass.

One leg was bent though flat on the mattress. Half contained, half open. Sexy, so sexy. With the tip of her fingernail she drew a line where the pale yellow sheet molded over his cock. Back and forth she traced until he began to swell. The sheet tented over his erection and her gaze roamed over his body as she continued to run her nail up and down.

"Wakey wakey, Lucas O'Connor."

His hand flexed and then his fingers wrapped around the narrow post in an oh-so-sexy move. Her heart pounded as she stared at his fingers. It was easy to imagine those fingers touching her but it was the way he held the headboard, as if in his dreams he was bound. There were so many little clues that he wanted bondage—his fingers gripping his wrist when he relaxed, his hand wedged within the headboard so he was imprisoned. If only she had brought rope or cuffs in with her.

Against her silk nightshirt her nipples swelled, aching in time with the tempo settling in her pussy. Up and down her fingernail traveled as his erection swelled more, the weight pulling him down to his belly. The fabric against the plump head grew damp.

She was damp, wet for him. Her hand slid under her shirt and she inhaled shakily when her fingers discovered how wet she was. Since she had understood her sexuality, she had wanted him like this. Even before she had realized she was a sexual Dominant, she had wanted him. To feel him fill her pussy, watch him orgasm as she rode him.

To have him submit to her without fear, without confusion. Her nail traced the vein on the underside of his cock, up and down as she traced her clit. The damp spot grew and she watched his eyes moving behind his lids. Was he dreaming of her? She wanted his thoughts to be consumed by her, like hers were of him.

Sitting on the bed, she watched his body jolt from the shift of his mattress. His eyes snapped open, awake but not alert. He blinked several times and she slid her foot along his body then rested it on his chest where his heart thumped hard from being jerked awake.

"Jess." His voice was raspy from sleep. His hand loosened on the post and she moved her foot so it rested against his fingers, holding them in place. Slowly he blinked and his grip tightened under her foot as he swallowed.

"I made a promise earlier," she said as she resumed the slow, teasing touch on his cock. He was adorable and sexy as he struggled to wake up, catching up with his oh-so-alert erection. "Do you remember?"

He licked his lips and his gaze slid along her leg to where the ends of her nightshirt hid her arousal from him. "A man isn't likely to forget."

Her finger touched the damp fabric, kissing the head of his cock. "I came," she said as her fingers curled around him.

Through the thin fabric she detected the frantic rhythm of his heart.

"Twice." Her grip tightened and she enjoyed the moan slipping from him as his hips pushed upward. Had there ever been such a sexy sound? "As I came, body shuddering and your name clinging to the air, I realized I wanted another one. Only I wanted you there."

He clutched the thin post so hard his knuckles turned white. The muscles in his arms strained and bunched as he met her gaze. So beautiful. Within her grip, his cock jerked, swelled and she rubbed the side with her thumb.

"I'm going to come but you can't. Not tonight." *Yes, Jessa, so glad you're not rushing him.* Perhaps if she resisted him, which she couldn't. "Do not let go and do not come." Her foot caressed down his forearm. "My will," she said and enjoyed the way his pupils dilated and how his cock swelled more in her grip.

Her foot slid under his biceps then with her free hand she eased her night shirt's buttons open. With only one hand, the process took a little longer but there was pleasure in drawing out the moment, in teasing him. "Tell me about this." She paused long enough to trace the horseshoe, enjoying the way his body tightened at the simple contact.

"A little luck never hurts."

Her nail scratched over the dark ink permanently marking him. "Luck can't hurt, but I do."

His pupils slowly dilated at her words. Sexy. Sexy was also the way his body rippled and stretched at the promise she made him in that minute. Oh, what she wanted to do to him.

"I'm so wet for you," she said in the quiet as she parted her shirt, baring her breasts, aching for his touch. "So wet." Her other leg draped over his stomach.

His mouth formed her name while his hand squeezed the wood harder.

"Do you want to see how wet I am?"

"Yes."

Her gaze focused on his face. "Yes, what?" Her fingers caressed her thigh even though everything within her went still. *This was it.* This was their point of no return. No more would there be any mistake or denial. Since the night at her studio, he had known exactly what she wanted.

This was their moment. Funny how nervous that made her feel. For so long she had wanted this and now here he was before her.

His pupils expanded as his hips surged up. "Yes, Mistress."

Holy. Hell. She almost came as the two words slipped from his mouth. "Don't you come," she ordered as she tightened her grip on him.

He cried out, arching up as her fingers clamped hard to keep him from coming.

"If you come, I won't give you the gift of watching me fuck myself for you." It was beyond erotic to watch his muscular body battle the need to climax and yet heed her order. Reaching into the pocket of her nightshirt, she removed the leather cock ring she had plucked from her little toy box in the studio.

The yellow sheet was almost transparent from pre-cum. Slowly she peeled it away, unveiling his swollen cock. "Fuck," he panted as she stretched the band wide then eased it over his swollen head. "Fuck!" Another bow of his body as she settled the elastic into place.

"Beautiful," she said as she stroked up the fabric, now snug against him. She caressed the engorged vein along the underside and enjoyed the way he jerked at the light touch. "You're so wet, baby." Leaning down, she kissed the damp, engorged head and he moaned, gripping her head with his free hand. "Grab the headboard."

Luke looked wild around the eyes as he tried to glare at her.

"I can leave." Her foot lowered to the floor and she shifted to balance on her other knee. Could she leave if he didn't? The internal question made her want to groan in frustration.

"No! No." He reached up, and his other hand slipped through the narrow posts, the wood pressed against the inside of his wrists.

"Where were we?" She caressed the jut of his hip bone.

He panted for air like one of the broncs after a hard ride, ribs rising and falling with each loud exhale. Her gorgeous, submissive cowboy. Yee-haw.

"You're wet," he said finally.

"Right. And I was going to show you. Right?"

"Yes."

Her eyebrow arched up.

He wet his lips. "Mistress."

Fuck, that word made her throb everywhere. "Look what you do to me," she said as she lightly stroked her fingers over her slick pussy. A gasp escaped her and she arched at the sensation before she leaned forward and painted her damp fingers over his lips. "This is for you, baby." Her finger slid into his mouth then returned to caressing the engorged penis she wanted inside of her.

He licked her as his hips rocked into her touch.

"You almost made me come," she said as she caressed his tongue, traced his mouth, "when you called me Mistress." She stroked her hand down his neck and rested over where his heart was pounding hard against his ribs. "Because I am, aren't I?"

"Yes," he whispered. "God, yes."

"Do you want me to fuck myself for you?"

"Jess," he breathed, his eyes closing.

"You look at me and answer." She milked his cock.

His tongue darted out to lick his lips but his eyes opened. They were glazed with arousal and submission. *Beautiful.* "No," he answered, his voice low and husky. "I want you to fuck me."

Smiling, she caressed up her thigh. His big body jerked as if an electrical current flowed through him. "But you don't get to fuck me tonight. You make me wish I had rope at this moment. And a crop. I want to watch how you react as I slash it against your ass. A virgin ass that's never been struck, yes?"

"Yes," he answered.

"Do you want me to?

His eyes closed again as if he was seeing it in his head. If only she could open up his brain, delve her hands within to see what he saw.

"God, yes, Mistress."

Her fingers found her throbbing clit and when she cried out, his eyes snapped open. "Watch me fuck myself for you, Luke. Know all this creamy wetness comes from seeing you like this. Know I anticipate each delicious thing I'm going to do to you. All for you," she said as she teased herself, moaning loudly when she found the aching fullness of her clit. His hips rocked up and down in time to her stroking hands.

Her finger eased into her pussy and they both arched, crying out in the room. Her eyes closed. She imagined it was him filling her instead of her finger, and she enjoyed him watching her. "Don't let go or I'll stop."

"Don't stop. Don't stop," he repeated again. "You're so beautiful, Jessa."

"All this cream," she eased a second finger in, "is because of you."

"Jessa."

Moaning softly, she fucked herself as she watched the dampness spread, his cock swell beneath her light touch. Arching, she buried another finger into her pussy, her gaze locked onto his hand holding the post. He shifted his hand. It bent behind the post, the back of his wrist against the wood while his fingers sought the other bar.

To keep from crying out she bit her lip. Her fingers pumped fast through the dampness and she stared at the wood against his wrist. Holding him immobile. Bound.

She met those blue eyes gazing at her with hunger and arousal.

Her hips jerked frantically and she arched. She came hard. Her cunt squeezed her fingers as cum spurted from her, drenching her hand and his sheet. "Luke," she cried out. A final spasm rippled through her aching, empty pussy as she came. Gasping she removed her shaking hand then brushed her fingers over his lips. Shifting, her lips whispered over his ear. "Luke," she breathed.

"Fuck me, Jessa. Please. Please fuck me."

She straddled his stomach and leaned down, kissing him as he begged her to take him. It was delicious, the sound of him, the body straining beneath hers. He didn't let go. Bless him, he didn't let go.

"Please," he whispered against her mouth. "Fuck me, Mistress. Let me come in you."

She caressed his cheek as she rubbed her wet pussy on his stomach. "I love hearing you beg, call me Mistress." Up his arms she traced to the hands holding onto the headboard as if they were the only thing keeping him on this bed. "But I'm not going to fuck you tonight."

He groaned her name and she hid her smile. "I'm not going to fuck you again until the fireworks. It's what you asked for." She rubbed over him as she nipped his lips with her own. "I will let you come though. And when you do, you will say my name." Bracing her hands on the pillow, she eased off him. She removed the cock band and eased the sheet off to admire him.

Man alive, he was beautiful. All hard muscle tight with arousal.

"May I let go?"

Curious as to where this was going, she nodded once. He let go of the rail and slowly sat up. His body trembled, his cock full and heavy as it leaked continuously. He kissed her then lifted her away from him.

Luke shifted to his knees and wrapped his strong hand around his cock. The tip was pressed to the wet spot left by her orgasm.

His hips circled while he held the plump, full head to the wet spot. His gaze met hers as his hand began to slide up and down. The rhythmic glide of those broad fingers working his thick cock was hypnotic. His thumb paused to trace the plump head while his fingers massaged over the vein. He was so beautiful, this creature kneeling before her. His eyes were closed and yet he never moved from the damp circle where she'd come. Harder he stroked, soft sounds emanating from him.

Jessa shifted onto her knees, mirroring his position. At the base of his throat she saw the frantic hammering of his pulse and heard the erotic sound of flesh sliding over flesh. She gazed down to watch his tanned hand then slowly up to the hard wall of his stomach, his chest where a drop of sweat slid towards his navel. His low moans made her stomach clench and her cunt spasm. He was so amazing. Leaning towards him she smelled the musky scent clinging to his skin and the heat of his body reached for her.

"Come," she whispered against his ear. A harsh, needy bark came from him and his large body jerked as if he had been struck. Or released from some inner bindings only he knew about.

"Mistress," he breathed as his cock emptied for her, paying homage to her orgasm.

She kissed him, feeling the shudders of his body as he came. It was beyond sexy. Not just him masturbating for her, or even needing her permission to come. All of him was sexy. That he had done this for her made something wrap around her heart. There had been other subs but none were Luke. His free hand slid under her shirt, covering her ass as he fed on her mouth, his tongue mating with hers.

He began to shake and she wrapped her arms around him, urging him down the bed. Curling against him, she caressed his sweat dampened face. His skin was hot to the touch as if he burned. She smiled and hummed to him, easing him through this moment.

"Stay," he whispered as she combed damp hair back from his forehead.

"I will."

He wrapped his arms around her, pulling her close. "Jessa."

"Sweet dreams, baby." Yes, this was her not rushing him at all. At. All. What if in rushing him he spooked again? There was so much she wanted to do with him, wanted him to experience. God, she was worried about repeating past mistakes. And yet it seemed impossible to go slow.

Way to stick to the plan, Jessa. Way to go.

Although if she had ignored the urge to slip into his room because of her promise to slow it down, she wouldn't be here, wrapped in Luke. At this moment, she couldn't think of a single place she'd rather be.

Chapter Seven

"I ALWAYS THOUGHT this was an easy process. You make it look as painful as getting kicked in the nuts by a bull."

Looking up from her notebook, Luke stood on the other side of the porch railing. He hooked his arms over the top and gazed at her with calm blue eyes. "Been kicked there a lot?"

"Thank hell, no. Come on."

"Where?"

"We're playing hooky." He shifted to the side so she saw two horses saddled and waiting.

Rising up, she set aside her guitar and walked over to him. With the height difference of the porch and where he stood, it made her a few inches taller than him. A girl had to like looking down on a guy once in awhile. He peered up at her, his hat pushed back on his head. "Are we?"

His fingers hooked in her front pockets and he nodded slowly.

"Think you'll get lucky?"

He smiled slowly.

Leaning down, she dipped her head under the brim of his hat. "But you asked for the fireworks." She kissed him because to not do so was a crime. "You said, 'Will you fuck me under the fireworks?' so that's what I'm going to do." She hadn't planned to stretch it out but torturing him was fun.

"Doesn't mean you can't do it beforehand." His hands shifted, flattening on her hips. "I ache, Jessa."

Her foot slipped between the posts and ran over his arousal, thick behind the denim. "I know."

He huffed at her smile. His fingers dug into her hips as her bare toes molded over his erection. She applied gentle pressure and the low, needy sound that escaped from him made all those hot, powerful impulses that begged to dominate this man surge to life.

They'd appear normal to anyone looking at them. Her standing on the porch as she talked to him. Only the two of them knew what she was doing. She pressed more against him. His fingers spasmed as his hips pushed forward into the contact, into the light pain. Oh how delicious. Through the denim of her cut-offs she felt the fabric grow damp from her response.

Her foot slid down the ridge of his fly, between the notch of his legs then down his thigh. Little pants came from him as he blinked a few times.

"I'll change."

"Pity," he said as he ran his legs down her bare legs, "to hide these legs. I dream of these legs, Jess. Wrapped around me, holding me close as I pound hard into you. I dream of them tightening around me as you come, shouting my name, as I spill into you. I *ache*."

His hands slid up under the ragged edges of her shorts to tease the crease where her thighs met her ass. Luke knew how to tease. She breathed heavily as his mouth formed the words, wove the image.

"I dream of these legs straddling my head as I quench the thirst of a lifetime on your pussy." His hands spread beneath the denim. "I *ache*, Jessa." His lips nipped hers. "I want inside you because I remember how good it felt to be there, to feel you come around me. I ache for *you*, Jessa. I always have."

When he kissed her, she felt shaky on the inside. His tongue boldly claimed her mouth, conquering with the hunger he had described. She fed on his mouth, craving him more than she had thought possible. Kissing Luke could sustain her for eternity.

Cupping his face, their lips clung together. The brim of his hat bumped against her head while the railing dug into her stomach. One of his fingers slid down, gliding along her wet, aching pussy. Her mouth broke away from his, panting as he touched her. Every time he touched her, it vibrated deep into her soul until she feared no one's touch would ever make her feel this hot, this special, this wanted.

"And now you ache for me. Come riding with me." His hands slid free and he sucked on his pinky.

"You're dangerous, O'Connor."

His eyebrows bobbed up and down. "You know what happens when you keep a man on the edge? He'll take you with him."

There was no "will take" when it came to him. She was right there with him, riding the hungry edge of need and passion. "I'll change."

"Oh no." He looked up at her, meeting her gaze. "Don't change for me, Jessa."

Sweet. He was sweet. She caressed his cheek, retrieved her guitar, then went inside to pull on her jeans and grab snacks. Her notebook mocked her while she pulled on her boots. They were playing hooky. Leaving it behind was part of the concept. With a frustrated curse, she shoved it and her well-chewed pencil into her small backpack, grabbed her hat and saw he had brought the horses up to the house.

She blew him a kiss. "Take me for a long, fast ride, Lucas."

"You kill me. You're totally killing me." He took her hand, kissed it, then helped her onto the horse.

Torturing him was fun. Spending time with him was a gift she had never anticipated. She wanted him to feel as alive as she did. A little grin curled his lips upwards and when he caught her looking at him, he winked. A smile glowed within because she knew he felt alive, too.

Thirty minutes later, they found a shaded area along the Bow River. Not far from where they relaxed in the shade of some balsam poplars, the horses were hobbled. Luke lay on his back, his head resting on her lap, relaxed and breath-taking. One of his hands was stretched over his head, his thumb hooked in her belt loop. The man was begging to be tied up. He was sexy in the saddle, as natural to him as breathing. It had been awhile since she had ridden. Not a lot of horses on tour. "I'm thinking of retiring my tour bus."

"Buying a plane?"

"Did you know I've basically been on the road since I was nineteen? Yes, there were down times, but there was always another tour."

His eyes opened and he gazed up at her. "You're retiring?"

"No," she said as she watched her horse daintily step into the river and take a drink. "I love the music too much to leave for good but touring... Yeah, I'd stop touring. A year on a bus with smelly boys or anonymous hotel rooms. It was suggested to me to buy a house before I bought here so I had a home base. A place to ground myself."

"Your place is here. I was told the same thing when I first hit the circuit. For me, it's the ranch. I help Dad out when I'm home, which I was once told was not down time. Like I was supposed to want to find a beach house and spend my time there. I don't surf, I don't want sand in my crack."

"Exactly." She gazed up at the blue sky beyond their little sheltered spot. "I've traveled the world, Luke. So many times. But I haven't seen it. And y'know, I don't really want to. I'm tired of the road. Do you ever get tired of it?"

"I've slowed down. A lot. I used to go to every rodeo. Chasing broncs. Now I only go to the rodeos that interest me. Ones not far from the ranch."

"Ones with a big pay out?"

"One-hundred thousand, Canadian. That's what? Five bucks American?"

She punched his chest and he laughed after a little

grunt. "I'll five bucks you."

His eyes glowed before he lowered his lashes. "Please. Do."

Smiling, she leaned back on her hands. "Fireworks."

He sighed as he shut his eyes. "You're so cruel."

She smirked up at the sky. "I know." Sinking down to her elbows, she liked the little grin on his face. "I really, really want to tie you up."

His eyes snapped open and he stared at the sky. His hand clenched on her belt loop.

"Have you ever been tied up?"

"No," he replied quietly.

She eased out from under him and stretched his arm above his head.

"You want to be, though. Did you know that when you sleep you trap your hand in the headboard rails? I noticed it last night. And at other times you'll clasp your wrists. Oh it looks all very casual and such, but..." She reached for his other hand and curled her hands around the strength of his wrists. "But you want them bound. It's like you're measuring the feel of something around your wrists."

He stared up at her, hunger burning in his gaze.

Her weight shifted onto his wrists, pinning him to the ground. "How has no one tied you up?"

His pulse leaped at his throat, his lips parted as he breathed deeper.

"How amazing would you be straining against the ropes? To see the fibers against your skin would be amazing. Held immobile as anticipation poured through you as you waited for my next move." Her thumbs caressed his wrists. She wanted that, too. To have him bound, to give him what he wanted. Suddenly, she was glad no one had tied him up before. She wanted to be the first to do that for him. One of her greatest joys, she realized, was giving Luke what he wanted.

"What would the next move be?"

"I'd kneel at your feet and slip a cock ring on you."

His lashes closed as his breathing grew a little raspier.

"Do you remember? Remember the way the elastics cinched around your cock. The pressure against your cock, the need to come and yet you can't. Then I'd take your beautiful cock into my mouth until you were fighting the ropes. To rip the ring from you so you could come, so you could get into me. I imagine you continuously leaking for me, cock heavy as I stand up to kiss you, so you can taste how much you need me." She looked down to see the bulge of denim. "Then I'd walk to your back. Your strong, muscular back.

"I have this crop. It's a favorite. Leather end. I love the sound it makes. Leather against flesh. A sharp snap. It would be delicious against all this hard muscle. Snap, pop, snap. Your ass, your thighs, your stomach, your balls."

He arched, and his thighs tightened as if they were about to be struck. Her hands caressed over the straining muscles because to not touch him was impossible. How far could she push him? Curious, she decided to see. Her hand glided up his thigh and she cupped his swollen cock.

"I'm taking you shopping before you leave."

"For what?" he whispered. A flush stained his cheeks and his hands fisted. The heel of her hand rubbed his cock, dragging a moan from him. Her own jeans were becoming damp from her arousal. How he made her wet.

"For a dildo." She covered his eyes with her other hand and felt the frantic fluttering of his lashes. His breath rasped in and out as she let him wonder why a dildo. There was, she admitted, no adhering to her original plan with him of going slow. Every instinct screamed at her to grab him and throw him down into the erotic fire of submission.

"A dildo?" His voice was ragged, his hips rocking into her massaging hand. Her hand slid from his eyes to the base of his throat where she felt the rapid beats of his heart.

"Do you trust me, Luke?"

At her questions his lashes ceased the nervous fluttering and his pulse rate steadied. Her own heart rate kicked up to the speed his had been hammering. He *trusted* her. It was a gift she had wanted all her Domme life. He hadn't trusted her five years ago. Not really. It's why he had freaked out, why he had flailed around and why, she admitted, his panic had hurt her.

Now he did. She wanted to ask when the trust had appeared but it was a dumb question. It's not like one marked it on their calendar. Trust was a truth you realized without realizing it.

"Yes," he whispered the word out. "Why a dildo, Mistress?"

Every time he called her that, her body tingled. She loved that he knew when to use the word and when to call her Jessa. It was like his trust. He knew without knowing. "It's the cock I'm going to use in your ass."

His eyes snapped open as his hips jerked. There was the flash of panic. How could one not feel a little concern at the thought of a cock going where you never thought of it going? But more than the panic, there was a flicker of curiosity. No repulsion, no denial. Just his pulse rate ratcheting up again.

"Oh, yes," she whispered. "I want you to walk in on your own, into a store vibrating with sex. I want the cock that makes your balls tingle and your ass clench as you imagine me sliding it into your ass. Hand on your stomach, breasts on your back as I fuck you."

"Jess." His hips rolled again as if he was imagining it. Her hand lowered to that tight rear of his, her finger tracing the ridge of the seam tucked in the tempting crack.

"Have you ever had your ass taken?" Even without him answering, she knew it was a no.

"No," he whispered.

"Oh, baby, have you done anything?"

"No."

Sweet God. She hadn't had a virginal submissive since her first. There was a blast of fear. She had fucked up so badly with her first sub, causing physical pain. But the panic was mild compared to the thrill of excitement building within. How she wanted to be the one to open up his eyes to all aspects of being a submissive. "How is that possible, baby?"

His gaze focused on her. "She wouldn't be you."

Her heart squeezed and she leaned down to kiss him. She felt...heartbroken. All those wasted years of her wanting to dominate him and him wanting to submit to her. Wasted, wasted time that she could've been showing him…*everything*. She kissed his forehead. "Lucas."

"You're sad. Why does that make you sad, Jess?"

He had spent how many years wanting this and yet denying it because it wasn't her.

Luke broke free easily enough and sat up, his hand sliding under her hair and tilted her head up. "Don't. Whatever you're thinking...don't," he whispered, his voice low and determined. He was submissive and sensitive but that didn't make him a pushover.

"How…" Jessa rested her forehead against his. "How?"

"I had a girl use handcuffs during sex." Luke pulled her forward, setting her onto his lap so his erection pressed against her. "Vanilla bondage. It was," he sighed as he cupped her ass, "not satisfying. I went to a few clubs but didn't participate. I watched, though."

Plucking a leaf from his hair, she flicked it aside. His hands flexed on her ass. Her hand pushed on his chest until he lay down and she lay on him, needing as much connection with him as possible. He looked away long enough to check on the horses, then stared into her eyes.

"There was a Domme, she reminded me of you even though she had blonde hair with pink strands. She was in this black latex outfit and had killer boots on. You ever wear that?"

"No," she laughed.

His face fell.

"I have leather."

His pupils dilated and his hands squeezed her ass hard.

"They're kind of like chaps but have a back, too, and

laces up the side that leave two inches of skin up the outside of my legs."

His hands caressed up her back as he rolled his hips up into her, his cock rubbing against her pussy that was so wet for him. Waiting until Friday seemed like the dumbest idea ever. Parting her legs was natural, rocking into the gentle grinding of his body was also natural. One his hands covered her ass again while she braced her own hands on the ground so she could see him.

"Leather bustier to match...complete with two-inch, laced up openings on the sides and front. The lacing is red leather, matching the trim of a cowboy hat. If I wear black leggings underneath and a camisole, it's suitable for public."

"Oh, God. I know that outfit. You wore it to the award show once," he moaned.

Slowly she kissed him, drinking down that sound. "Tell me about your Domme."

"Not mine," he growled, making the distinction known. The anonymous Domme he had watched wasn't his. Jessa was. She glowed internally at the thought. Would it spoil her bad-ass reputation to pump her fists in the air with a shouted yahoo?

"Her sub was on a St. Andrew's cross, cuffs at his wrists, ankles and thighs. She had her whip wrapped around her waist and she unwrapped it slowly as she stood behind him. Like she was uncoiling a boa constrictor from her waist. She whipped him and fuck, Jess."

His eyes closed as he slowly thrust against her. "It was so erotic the way she marked him. Every snap of her whip, my cock throbbed. She walked to him and had another sub help slip a harness on her, the dildo black to match her outfit. I watched her penetrate him, her hands almost gentle as she took him. I nearly came right then. She fucked him, rode him until he almost came and then she pulled out of him, took her whip and lashed him again. Over and over she repeated this. I wanted, Jessa. I wanted so badly for that to be me. For her to be you."

Resting her forehead against his, she ached at the pain buried in his voice, pure want. And she was scared to rush him? How silly they both had been over the past years? Denying each other their deepest desires. And why? Because they were scared? What a couple of idiots. "I let you suffer for five years, didn't I?"

"Yes." His hands fisted in her hair as he pushed against her as if stopping was impossible. The conversation, the memories, whatever was playing in his mind, was arousing her cowboy. A lot. This was a conversation they should've had years ago. Lost time was so stupid. "That day in my trailer. I didn't know it was in me. Well, there was that fucking spur way back when, but I didn't know what it was I was craving. Did you? Did you know what was hidden in me?"

She braced a hand on the ground. She couldn't lie to him. "Yes," she answered softly.

"How? When?"

"The spur." She leaned down. "I followed you."

"And you did nothing? Nothing?"

"Please. I was a kid. I had no understanding at all. But I knew it was there." Easing away from his thick erection, she decided it was time for her own honesty.

This world they lived in was based on trust. It was

unfair for him to be the only one sharing his truths. His chest rose and fell with his hard breaths and she caressed him until he wasn't clinging to the edge by his teeth.

She eased off him, though kept her leg over him. Needing the contact "You remember how I said wasn't so touchy-feely?"

Sitting up, his hands rested on her thighs. Her head eased to his shoulder and she listened to the river not far from them.

"Yes," he said in a quiet voice, the same tone he had used on Prince Charming when he had been pissed about having a saddle put on him. Nothing like being treated like a nervous horse to boost a girl's ego. Granted it was soothing. As if everything would be okay just because his voice said so.

"I hurt my first submissive. Badly. I didn't know what I was doing. I was nineteen, my hormones were out of whack. My fantasies were...intense. Pain, sex, it was all entwined in my mind. It's why I wasn't touchy-feely." She lifted her head and met his gaze. His fingers combed through her hair and she returned her head to his shoulder. It was a great place to be...safe. Leaning against his strong body as she confessed her past made her feel protected. "It was hard to want to kiss a guy when you saw yourself hurting them and you didn't understand it. But then..."

"Tell me what happened?"

"We were experimenting and I didn't know about limits or how to do anything. I hurt her. She didn't know anything either. We were kids."

"Wait. Her?"

Jessa had to smile at the way he went still and alert. Men. "If you're about to experiment with your sexuality, you want it to be with one you trust. Explicitly. She was discovering hers, I was discovering mine…"

"Robin Mathers," he said quietly, guessing correctly. "Your first submissive was Robin? That's so hot. So god damn hot." He cleared his throat then brought the conversation back to the point. "How'd you hurt her?"

She played with his fingers as she exhaled. "Robin has a scar on her back because I had no idea what I was doing. I drew blood. I hit her hard. Hard enough to break skin. Hard enough to scar. She came along on my first tour. A couple of girls having an adventure. It was so thrilling, the music part and one night we were in my room on the bus and we got to talking the way you do. From talking we went to trying. From trying it went to me hurting her. I was so scared. Screamed for Mason Griffon for help because she was bleeding. I didn't mean to hurt her but when you don't know what the hell you're doing…"

"Jess," Luke whispered as he wrapped her in his arms, a haven for her. Robin had said she was vulnerable in regards to Luke. She was, but he was also sturdy so when she was feeling vulnerable, he was the strength. It was nice, comforting. Like the hand lightly rubbing her back and the kiss pressed against the top of her head.

"Griff called us idiots as we sat in the emergency, Rob getting stitches. 'You don't get on a horse and ride. You learn. You don't fly a plane the first time you sit in the pilot chair. You learn. You fucking learn and you be fucking responsible, Jessa Mae.'" She sat up and pointed a finger at Luke while glaring, imitating the lecture Griff had yelled at her. Luke took her hand, nipped her finger. She sighed. "So, I learned. He made me be submissive."

Luke laughed despite the serious conversation. "Your lip so curled."

"I am not a good submissive but I learned. I saw it through her eyes, and I learned. I learned how to make the pain about pleasure and wow...orgasmic. He taught me the right tools, the right methods and I learned." Moving to his lap, she needed to surround herself with him. His hands curled over her hips. "But I hurt her. I would've hurt you."

Jessa traced his mouth with shaking fingers. Hurting Robin had hurt, had ripped her heart out. Hurting him would've been the same. Perhaps worse. Because, as Rob said, she was vulnerable in regards to him.

"And you didn't know what you wanted. How much would it have freaked you, Luke? Maybe enough you would've hated me, maybe enough you vowed to never do it again, which would've been a crime. No, I couldn't do anything then because neither of us was ready."

"You didn't do much later, either."

"A little cock and ball torture freaked you out, Luke. You were freaked. It was in your eyes. The 'what the fuck was that?' look, even though you liked it. You lashed out because I opened a door I didn't know was closed. Had I, I probably would have handled it better."

"And now I know."

"Now you know." Leaning down, she kissed him. Snagging the bottom of his shirt, Jessa drew it up to reveal the muscles etched into his stomach. Her fingers splayed over his abdomen to feel the taut skin. Touching him was no longer a compulsion she had to fight. How amazing that all the hard strength was covered by almost satiny skin.

A nipple pebbled beneath her exploring fingers and his eyes narrowed in pleasure at being petted. Even the dark hairs at his arm pits were sexy because they were him.

She stroked up his arms, dragging the body-hugging black shirt up and away so he was shirtless. Her heart gave a few extra thumps at seeing him before her. She'd need a giant thesaurus to find the right word to describe all his masculine beauty.

Flattening a hand on his chest, she pushed him down so he was lying on the ground. "Hands over your head. Wrists together."

He obeyed and she pulled off her tank top and her bra.

"Jess."

She traced up his arms, enjoying the round firmness of his muscles and the easy way he capitulated. When she leaned over him, his captured her nipple in his mouth. His tongue flicked the tight bud while he sucked hard and a moan escaped from her. Jessa wrapped her bra around his wrists and this time he moaned. She folded the bottom of her tank up then again before she covered his eyes.

"Open your mouth." She slid the straps in his mouth. His nostrils flared when he couldn't see her. Leaning down, she licked one of his flat nipples. When it beaded she bit him, hard. Luke gave a muffled bark as he arched up.

"You're so strong, pure athletic grace." She sought the second nipple and enjoyed the way he surged up beneath him when she bit him again. "It's what makes your sexual submissiveness so hot." She licked a scar, kissed it then licked and sucked her way over the hard muscles of his belly.

"An amazing body. You were hot as a rather skinny teenager, but all filled out you are beyond gorgeous." His erection pressed between her breasts and a shaky sigh escaped her to feel his arousal nestled there, hardness between softness. If he was naked, she'd feel the heat of his skin, the beat of his heart. As she gazed up the long, lean line of him, his hands fisted at his cock being trapped between her breasts.

"So many assume the sub is weak, the Domme is strong. We're strong because you make us that way. Your trust in us not to hurt you—as we hurt you—makes us stronger." Her tongue dipped into his belly button and she looked up at him, his wrists tied in lace. "You should look foolish with pink lace wrapped around your wrists but you don't. You look sexy and masculine. I think it makes you stronger, how you submit." Her hand traced along the rough denim of his waistband. His skin was heated satin against the pad of her finger.

"The control you have. Oh, the control not to come until I say so. That's strength. To stand, or kneel, or be cuffed while I flog you...that's strength. No," she said as she rubbed her cheek over him, enjoying the ragged moan from him. "Those who don't see are blind. So blind." Unbuckling his belt she slowly pulled it from the loops. She rubbed the bronze buckle over his stomach.

"Pick a word. One you'd never accidentally say during sex." She reached up and eased the wet fabric from his mouth. "And not stop."

Shifting down to his feet she pulled off his cowboy boots and socks. They were set aside then she turned around to face him once more.

"Halt." His voice was low and raspy with desire.

Jessa opened the button on his jeans. "Halt. I like it." She kissed his stomach. "If I do anything that causes more pain than pleasure, you say halt. If I do anything that freaks you out, you say halt. It's your safe word." Easing the zipper over the impressive swell of his cock she peeled his jeans off.

"Leaking," she said when she saw the wet spot on his shorts. His shorts were stripped off then she folded his jeans. "On your knees. However you can, I want you on your knees, hands on your head."

Gracefully, he rolled into position. The joys of a natural born athlete. "Up. There are rocks." The jeans were tucked under his knees when he shifted. She adjusted the makeshift blindfold over his eyes.

Naked he knelt there, blindfolded, wrists bound and fingers locking together like a lifeline.

"Oh, Luke." She crouched in front of him. "Do you know how magnificent you are kneeling, your cock thick and hard, your wrists bound?" Kissing him she stroked his cock then reached for the belt. Holding the buckle, she wrapped the belt around her hand twice then gazed at this gorgeous man.

The leather stroked across his chest, scraping one

nipple with the belt's edge, and he gasped. His nipple tightened, the muscle twitching beneath golden skin. She enjoyed the sight so much she scratched the other nipple. This time with the bronze buckle. His hands squeezed tight as his mouth parted.

The hard plain of his stomach drew taut as she caressed the leather down. At the base of his throat, his heart pounded as hard and fast as hers. His breathing came faster the lower she drew the belt. "Don't come," she ordered. "What you'll miss if you do."

He was beautiful as he fought for control, his head tilted down as if he saw through the blindfold. Her hand wrapped in the leather bypassed his engorged cock, the tip weeping pre-cum. Each little hair on his thigh seemed to rise as the belt slid down to his knees, his muscles quivering. His entire body vibrated in anticipation, in fear of the unknown.

It was intoxicating.

Her panties soaked while her nipples throbbed at the sight of this strong male on his knees. She caressed the belt up his other leg and enjoyed his soft oath as his head fell back. His knuckles were white around the shirt and his arms shook.

"Nervous?"

"No," he panted out.

She pressed the belt against his testicles and his entire body went tight. "Nervous now?"

"A little."

"Remember, you aren't allowed to come." Grinning, she dragged the crisp edge of the belt along his cock. He swore and his thighs tightened as if that alone would keep him from climaxing without permission.

Exhaling slowly, her breath was shaky in her chest. This was it. No previous Domme experience topped this moment. All because it was Luke.

Standing she walked around him. His ass snapped tight, the muscles jumping beneath the skin. He was so going to pop.

She leaned down and relished the bead of sweat trickling down his temple. Sexy. "The first one always hurts, but you always remember it"

"The first what?"

There was no warning as she slapped the brown leather over his ass. He came immediately as he shouted. Cum spurted everywhere, coating the ground before him, dripping from his cock that wasn't as hard now but wasn't soft either.

"Fuck," he rasped out. Her own breath feathered out as her pussy contracted and she came at the sight of him. Claiming his mouth, she enjoyed the way it clung to hers as their tongues glided together.

"I thought I said not to come."

Five more times she struck him and she loved the way his ass tightened and turned red. She caressed his cheek, almost the same shade as his ass. Her big, beautiful cowboy shook as she walked around him. Her fingers combed through his hair. With the wrapped leather around her hand, she nudged his head and claimed his mouth once more, marking him inside and out.

"You totally made me come," she said against his lips.

He pulled away and pressed his face against her stomach. His fisted hands fell to his lap as if all the strength had been depleted with his orgasm.

Luke sank down and hissed when his tender ass rested on his heels. Straddling his lap, she wanted to touch him, taste him. The bra was untangled from his wrists and Jessa stripped off the blindfold. He blinked at the sudden light then his hand fisted in her hair as he devoured her mouth.

Down his back she caressed and returned the hungry kiss. It was a sensual battle of lips and tongues. Her fingers drew lines up his arms, the muscles still twitching from being held over his head.

"You're wet."

"I'm soaked," she corrected. Smiling, he lowered his head to her breasts. He delivered a soft kiss as his hands lightly ran down her back to her hips. She was aware of them shaking.

"Jessa,'" he whispered as he wrapped his arms around her, his hand spreading on her back. "I didn't...I..."

Resting her cheek on his hair, she stroked his back. Tears blurred her vision as she sensed dampness on her breasts. Five years, she thought with an ache. There was torture and then there was putting a mirror in a man's face and not being around for the fallout. Beyond irresponsible. Griff would have her ass. Her arms tightened around him and she vowed never again. Never would she leave him wanting. Needing? Yes. Aching? Absolutely. Wanting? No.

"Sleep with me tonight," she said in the quiet. Never had she slept with a man. Fucked them? Yes. Fallen asleep with them? No. This was an intimacy...one reserved for him.

"You want to torture me. When is it Friday?"

"Two sleeps."

A heavy sigh came from him. "That's *for*ever."

She smiled slightly. "There's a grassy spot in the sun." She kissed his head. "Let's get you out of the shadows."

After she helped him to his feet, they walked to the spot she had picked out for him. He was utterly comfortable naked. Good thing, as she planned on keeping him nude for awhile. He sank to his knees as if the walk took all his strength. With a groan, he belly flopped forward.

"And that was only six strokes of a belt. Small potatoes compared to what I want to use on you." She gently stroked his back then his ass. One still-red cheek received a sharp slap then she leaned down to kiss his shoulder. "I'll be back."

Retrieving her notebook and pencil, Jessa joined him. He was asleep and murmured when she slipped his shirt over his hips. An arm hooked over her crossed legs, and his hand slipped under her thigh. She caressed his arm, opened up her book and then began to write.

Chapter Eight

THE SOUND OF children and adults mingled with the various animals on exhibition in the agricultural building. The air had the familiar musty scent of animal, hay and stale popcorn. Did she want a Clydesdale at her place? The question revolved around her mind as she stroked the velvety nose of a dark Clydesdale. Perhaps she needed a barn and a house before she started thinking of what was going to live with her there, but that was really semantics.

She and Luke were going to meet up here. She hadn't wanted to hang around the gate like some buckle bunny. Only one of the rodeo cowboys interested her and that was Luke O'Connor. The very same Luke O'Connor who had won the day's ride.

The very same Luke O'Connor she had delighted in denying for three days. Three days of teasing him. Three days of withholding permission for him to come. Three days since she had introduced his ass to his belt. Three days of craving him within her.

She felt like a hormonal sex addict because in denying him what he wanted, she wasn't getting what she wanted.

Oh, the double-edged sword of torture. She could come and she had by her hand, his hand, his mouth, but it had a bittersweet tang to it because it was only her. Did she get off on him begging for release? Yes. Oh yes. Touching him, kissing him, and torturing him, however, only made her crave the feel of him within her body even more.

Addict indeed.

She was a Lucas junkie.

Hands settled on her hips and she smiled without looking away from the horse. "Hello, cowboy," she said as his touch slid to her stomach. Gently, he kissed the back of her neck and her stomach made a jumpy motion. The same jittery feeling had moved through her when she had looked at Luke sitting on top of the bronc awhile ago, an utter look of concentration on his face.

"Making a new friend?"

"Naturally." His fingers dipped under the bottom of her tube top, the color a coppery metallic that she had purchased on her shopping spree with Robin. Her skin tingled where he touched and her breathing got a little shaky. "Not the place, O'Connor."

"I want in you, Jessa." His voice was low against her ear, his breath a puff of heat on her skin. "You have no idea how badly I want in you. I want to push this little, bitty denim skirt up over your ass and bury myself in you."

His lips danced over the back of her neck as he talked, need giving the words an extra layer of heat. Her hands curled over the wooden gate and her vision lost focus so the horse was simply a dark blur. Against her ass she felt the hard press of his erection.

His words, his touch, his voice, his presence made her wet and the little swatch of her panties grew damp as he aroused her with his words and his need. The sharp lines of his belt buckle dug into her back and she wondered if the graphic etched on the metal would be imprinted on her skin...like he was.

"I need in you," he whispered into her ear. "Let me come in you. Let me fuck you. I *ache*, Mistress."

A shaky sigh exploded from her. He turned her, pulling her close against his hard body and claimed her mouth in a sizzling kiss. Clutching his shoulders, her legs were weak from his declaration. His tongue stroked over hers in bold hungry licks. The brim of his cowboy hat knocked against hers, threatening to send it to the hay strewn floor. The noise surrounding her faded away as he devoured her mouth. A hand rested on her thigh, inching up under the back of her skirt. He traced the line where her leg met her ass and she broke the kiss, half concerned he was going to get them arrested at the Stampede.

His blue eyes seemed to burn with pent-up sexual needs and adrenalin from his ride. An answering tug burned within her. Her heart thundered so hard in her chest she wondered if the rest of the world could hear it. "If that hand goes up any higher, cowboy, we're in a lot of trouble."

"Need *you*," he said, his jaw clenched around the words. His hips bumped forward. "*Now.*"

Her poor, tortured submissive cowboy was on the edge of losing utter control. If he was aware they were smack dab in the middle of the Stampede grounds, it was not reflected in his gaze or his words. She caressed his cheek, the touch soothing them both

"Know this, Lucas," she warned in a low voice that went no further than the space between them, "I *can* make you come right now."

His eyes closed as a shudder moved through him.

"I can release you this very moment but if I do, know that you don't get to fuck me later on."

A muscle in his jaw flexed and she swore she heard teeth grinding.

"Move. Your. Hand. Now."

Not that she wanted that hand off her. She wanted to drag him down to the ground so he could unleash all that energy within her. One of them, however, had to maintain control of the situation or they'd wind up in jail.

His sigh sounded more like an angry animal than man as he eased his hand out from under her skirt. He continued to hold her pinned against him, his erection prodding her through their clothing. Luke turned his face into her hand and he took a deep breath as if reigning in his control. Foolish man, he had none. She wouldn't let him keep it.

Luke kissed her palm then rubbed his face down her arm before burying it in her neck. Stroking the back of his neck, she massaged the tight muscles. "So how much of this is me and how much is from that ass-kickingly fantastic ride?"

Against her neck, he smiled.

"That was one helluva ride, baby." He straightened at her words and sent her a grin that was pure boyish delight. "Going for the top spot?"

Luke gave her a hard kiss, maintained a grip on her

waist and arched back as he released a loud whoop. She laughed, enjoying his joy in today's ride. Hugging him was as natural as teasing him.

"Oh it was sweet. Wasn't it sweet?"

He had clung to his bronc with the same grit and determination he showed when struggling against her command for him not to come. He was tenacious.

"You need food. You haven't eaten since early." They had left the ranch at dawn so they could go the parade. They could've arrived later but it was all about finding the right spot to watch everything. A spot with grass had been found and armed with a thermos of her mom's coffee, they had waited for nine o'clock to arrive and the parade marshal for the official start of the Stampede.

To pass the time, Luke had stretched out beside her, his head in her lap, his hat on his face, keeping out the sun and had napped. Being with him made it easy to forget there was the world outside Jessa Brody. Within minutes of claiming their primo parade watching spot, she had been recognized. At the first stuttering of, "Are you Jessa Brody?" Luke had sat up, as if distancing himself from her. On her parents' ranch, it was easy to forget there was this. There she was Jessa or Mistress. Out here she was Jessa Brody.

There had been some relief when the parade started. Approaching her had become more complicated as people lined up and down Ninth Avenue. One of the local news channels had spotted her and she missed a few of the marching bands as she was interviewed. Luke sat beside her and yet it had felt like a chasm opened up between them. She'd bet anyone watching the news later wouldn't realize she had come with Luke O'Connor, bronc rider. That annoyed her. She wanted everyone to know he was hers.

"Ah, I feel fucking awesome." Luke wrapped an arm around her chest and yanked her back, dipping her to kiss her. "You taste sweet. You had cotton candy."

Blushing, she felt as if she'd been caught doing something she shouldn't have. "Pull me up before someone sees what I'm wearing under my skirt." Drawing her up he took her hand, his fingers entwining with hers. "What do you want to eat?"

"You." Lifting her hand, he lightly bit the back of her thumb. A zing of heat flowed from her thumb to her pussy, detouring through her heart.

Jessa thumped his chest with the back of her hand playfully. "That's dessert."

"I love dessert. It's my favorite meal." When he stopped walking, the hold Luke had on her had brought Jessa to a stop. He tilted her hat back on her head then cupped her face in his hands.

Gazing up at him, she realized that there was sense of disbelief that she was here with him. The last time they were at a rodeo things had gone so terribly wrong. And now here was this beautiful, sexy man painting her lower lip with his thumb. How had that happened? What planets had aligned to bring him not just back into her life but into her world?

His head lowered and as soft as the sun shining down on them, he kissed her. Within her strappy sandals, her toes curled as she covered his hands, savoring the gentle glide of his lips over hers while people flowed around them.

The kiss ended and this time she was the one to turn her head and nip his thumb. "Food, cowboy. You need your strength." She liked the way his nostrils flared as he inhaled, the sharp sound his breath made. The tiny bite wound was nurtured with a little lick then she took his hand and led the way to the nearest food kiosk.

There was no shorter line-up nearby and the thought of wandering around the grounds trying to find a shorter line hurt her head. The goal was to feed him, not waste time. There was a promise to fulfill within a couple of hours.

He stood behind her, so close she felt the heat of his body reaching for her. A finger traced the top of her tube top and a giggle escaped at the ticklish touch. "Stop it." Turning, she swatted at him then moved forward. He moved with her. Between the waistband of her skirt and the bottom of her top the soft glide of his finger brushed along her again.

This time she didn't turn but reached behind her to brush away his hand. "Stop it."

A low chuckle came from him. Once more along the top seam, his finger made a slow journey. "I swear, if you don't stop, I'll—"

"What?" His voice was low and close to her ear. "You'll what?"

"I will tie you up and beat you until you beg for mercy."

Behind her, Luke went still and then very slowly, very blatantly brushed his finger along her shoulders.

"Promises, promises," Luke whispered behind her.

It was one promise she intended to keep.

"Are you Jessa Brody?"

The teasing caress came to a halt. Against her spine she felt the tip of his finger and it was like a gun about to go off. She could lie but that always came back to bite her in the ass. "Yes," Jessa answered, utterly conscious of that finger pressing and pressing. Instinct had her reaching back with her left hand to hold him place, to keep him close.

"Oh my God," the two girls breathed. They had to be seventeen or eighteen. "Oh. My. God!" The last word was a high-pitched shriek that only teenage girls seemed to pull off. They began to ramble, a battering vocal combination of words. She tried to translate, she really did, but all she was aware of was that finger on her spine and the stillness of Luke.

There was a little shift but it was as if there had been an earthquake, the removal of his weight as he stepped away. His touch vanished and she became highly aware of his absence. She glanced back to make sure he was still there.

For half a heartbeat their gazes met and then he looked away. Something loosened within and she felt like she had been sent careening away. Word spread fast thanks to the continuous flow of words from the two girls. Griff had once described it as the star virus. You could be invisible one minute but the minute recognition hits, everyone sees you. Your secret identity has been stripped away by the immunity virus.

"Would you sign..." The first girl looked around as if realizing she had nothing worth signing. "Anything?"

A pen appeared as if by magic.

Luke took a step sideways then another. The distance spanning between them grew. She signed a napkin the girl's friend had retrieved. Then another napkin, someone's hat, someone's paper cup that had once housed fries before they had upended it. She could've signed anyone's name for all the attention she gave the people. Luke was all that mattered and that distance.

It was getting wider and she wanted to scream in frustration. He wandered over to a kiosk where someone was selling leather goods. The minute his back turned something broke apart inside her.

Time to go.

She eased out of the cluster of people. It could escalate soon and all she wanted to do was leave. To go home and lick the wounds that had suddenly appeared. He was admiring an embroidered wallet and she wondered how much of it he saw.

"Let's go," she said, unable to look at him because then he would know.

"Finished?"

Blinking, she wondered if he meant more than the impromptu autographing session was finished.

Griff had warned her. Repeatedly. Not about this exactly but about this kind of situation, that her different worlds could never be in the same orbit.

Funny. Never once since *Tempt Me* had hit the airwaves had she thought it would be like that with Luke. She had assumed it would be like Robin—natural. Robin knew all the facets of her but she also knew that at the core she was always Jessa Mae Brody.

How many times, a childish part of her thought, would he pull away from her? How many times was this going to happen, where she thought they were moving forward only they weren't? How many times did he need to reject some piece of her?

She was unprepared for the hurt. Had she forgotten what it felt like five years ago to have him inflict wounds from his own fears? Or had it not just felt like someone had reached into her and ripped out something vital?

"Yes," she finally said softly. "I'm finished."

They walked in silence to his truck, joining the mass exodus of the Stampede grounds.

"Jessa?"

Shaking her head, she struggled against what had just happened. "Just take me home."

"What?"

"Home." How far had they parked? The walk seemed to take forever. Was she leaving a blood trail behind? "It's not real you know."

"What?"

She waved a hand over her shoulder. "That. It's not real." Where was his god damn truck?

"I know."

Stopping, Jessa looked at Luke. He continued then halted when he realized she wasn't with him.

"Do you, Luke? Because from where I was standing, you didn't." He had walked away. Again.

"I was just giving you privacy."

"Bullshit," she said quietly. "Bullshit." His body had slid away from her until her hand had no choice but to fall emptily to her side. "Bull-fucking-shit." Poking him the chest, she stared up at him. "That wasn't you giving me privacy. That was you—" *walking away*. She couldn't say the words.

If she said them out loud, they became true.

"I want to go home." She wanted her own world around her when she shattered. Glaring, she looked around. "Where is the damn truck?" How could she make him understand? "You walked away, Luke."

"Jessa—"

"You didn't step aside. You walked away." Confusion showed in his eyes. "This isn't real, Luke. It's a dream. A hallucination. I'm not real to them. They see 'Jessa Brody,' not me. I don't want them to. If you can't see that then I guess you don't see me. *See me*, Luke, not the dream."

"Jessa—"

"It's just another facet of me. I'm an all or nothing kind of girl, Luke. You take all of me, even fans who want me for two seconds, or none of me."

"I'm not going to…"

"To what? Give them that two seconds? Let me have that two seconds?"

He yanked off his cowboy hat and raked a hand through his hair. The realization was coming now. That this was going to happen all the time. Her name hit the gossip papers once in awhile. No doubt someone would wonder about the man spotted with her at the parade *and* the grounds. "She's overwhelming. She's this famous person. She's—"

"Me," she said quietly "Jessa Mae Brody, Jess, Jessa Brody, Mistress, they're *all me*, Luke. Don't compartmentalize me. That's not fair. Halt." The word slipped from her.

He blinked, confused.

Jessa flattened her hand on his chest, absorbed that contact with him. "Halt."

She saw the churning of his brain as he realized what the word was. His safe word. To stop her when she did something that scared him or hurt him beyond pleasure. Not since Griff's training days had she uttered a safe word. Her hand fell.

They stared at each other. It was time for them to stop hurting each other.

"Jessa." His voice broke and his hand fisted at his side. "Don't."

"You think I didn't see you pull away at the parade when I was recognized? That you didn't pretend to not know me? You're always pulling away when things become hazy. So I'm clearing things up. Halt, Lucas. Halt."

What the hell had just happened?

Luke squeezed the steering wheel as he looked at Jessa staring out the window of his truck. It had been the worst drive of his life. The joy of his ride this afternoon was gone, wiped out by the panic that he had fucked up again. There was giant bus parked in the Brody yard. "Jessa, don't do this. I'm sorry. This is not a world I know."

A guy with blond hair jumped down from the Brodys' front porch. Even from inside the truck they heard his exuberant whoop.

"I never thought it would be my job that would make you pull away." Jessa's voice was soft and husky. "I always thought it would be something I did to your body. It's a job, Luke. It's just a job. A little high profile but it's what I do. Not who I am." Opening the door she slid out. "You know what I thought this entire ride home? What will make him retreat from me in the future? What part of me will he reject next?"

Don't, he thought with panic. *Don't close the door.*

A soft click echoed through his head. The guy grabbed Jessa and lifted her up, spinning her around. He tried to remember the guy's name. Jessa eased away and Luke strained to hear her voice through the glass.

Shit. His hands strangled the steering wheel as he watched her head towards the house. An older guy wearing jeans and a white T-shirt was approaching Jessa. When they reached each other, he caught her chin, tilting her head back. A hard look was aimed at Luke. There was no mistaking the way his hand formed a fist and how he was envisioning using it on Luke's face before he took Jessa's arm and guided her toward the bus instead of the house. They vanished inside and he sat in his truck.

How had everything had gotten so fucked up so badly?

More importantly, how did he fix this?

No answer came and there was no time to ask her because the next person he saw step off the porch was his own dad.

The invasion had begun.

He'd sneak into her room tonight to fix this. Somehow, some way.

Only she had given up her room for his parents and sequestered herself in her studio. Rehearsal. That's what everyone said.

Luke knew the truth.

She wanted nothing to do with him. They had been secluded on the ranch pre-Stampede. There it was easy to forget she was Jessa Brody—Superstar. She was simply Jessa Brody unless it was just the two of them and then Mistress would creep out. Both drove him wild. Jessa Brody—Superstar, not so much.

And she knew it.

Was this thing with Jessa forever doomed? They didn't even live in the same country. If she stopped touring, he couldn't even slap down his credit card and join the hordes of people who watched her perform. More than once he had done that. Like a closet stalker, he had sat in his chair and watched her tear up the stage with her voice then he'd go home alone with his emotions wrecked.

More, he thought with panic. He wanted more than those stolen glimpses or this past week. Was it him or had she said the same thing? Confusion and hopelessness battered at him. Halt was the worst four-letter word in the world.

Chapter Nine

THE ROAR OF the crowd felt muted in his head, as if plugs were jammed deep in his ears. Feet pounded the metal stairs surrounding the floor space where the hockey ice rink normally was while thousands of people shouted Jessa's name. There was a ringing in his head from the earlier music and something hot was squeezing in his chest at having watched her perform.

He and their two families were in the front row. When he had entered almost two hours ago, he had expected to be asked to leave. "Sorry, Mr. O'Connor, you broke Jessa Brody's heart for the second time. Please get the fuck out."

Back and forth she had walked across the stage, singing her sultry, sexy songs wearing skin licking black leather pants and a denim vest that showed off the stomach he had worshipped. Not once had those rich, dark eyes looked at him. Her concert had ended with her biggest hit, *Tempt Me* as the encore. To him the song had seemed sad, haunting like she had reached down into him and ripped out all his vital organs so he was nothing but an empty shell.

Luke stared at the concrete floor between the toes of his boots, everything ached inside because why?

He was a coward that was why. When it came to his Jessa, he was a total chicken shit.

The Saddledome erupted into screams and he looked up to watch Jessa walk out with her guitar. Mason Griffon followed. Griff who had wanted to hit him but hadn't. Luke still saw that hand curl into a fist, still saw those hard black eyes judge him as unworthy before the older man had walked away.

They sat down on two stools, their bodies slightly angled towards each other. The two knew how to command the stage. Did anyone else see that power? He felt it on his skin as it seeped through pores and spread through him until his entire body tingled. It was as if a wave fanned out from where they sat. One that demanded utter silence.

Did anyone realize it was the dominant in them? The very core of power that made him want to give them everything, give her everything. Griff's foot tapped soundlessly against the floor while Jessa's moved in sync from where it was hooked on the lowest rung of her stool.

A steady heart beat came next as Griff tapped his hand against his guitar. *Pfwump-pfump.* Pause pause. *Pfwump-pfwump.*

Luke knew Griff was on the stage but all he saw was Jessa, her head bowed so he studied the crown of her cowboy hat. There was a rhinestone band around it, at the front there was a jeweled rendition of the Brody brand.

"Everywhere I go, I look."

As if he was on a descending plane, there was a soft

pop in his ears and then nothing was muted anymore. Luke heard her husky voice clearly, heard the soft tap-tap from Griff's guitar. Then she picked up the rhythm from Griff. Two hearts beating in silence. His own began to ache.

"*Everywhere I am, I seek. Every place I see, I search. Everywhere I roam, I wonder.*"

Her fingers flexed over the strings and the note vibrated deep within him. He knew that note. How many times had he heard it as muttered curses spilled from her?

"*Where do you go when I can't see you? How do you feel when I can't touch you? Why are you hiding, my prairie blue?*"

Griff joined in playing the melody that had been coming from Jessa's guitar since she had arrived at her parents' home. Had it always sounded that haunting and sad? He couldn't remember but he was pretty sure the answer was no.

Luke wanted to leave, to stand up and walk out because this was wrong. This was Jessa unplugged. This was Jessa vulnerable. This was Jessa raw. His heart felt jittery with each word she sang. His hearing seemed to come and go as he looked at the woman on stage.

"*It's all spinning crazily out of control. I'm out of step, out of sync, as you're out of reach. Why are you hiding, my prairie blue?*"

Jesus. Fuck. Bracing his elbows on his knees, he hunched forward, his gaze locked on Jessa. *Even the strongest bleed, son.* His dad had said that once when one of his toughest bulls had been injured because some assholes had dumped old barbed wire in one of their pastures and the male had stumbled into the mess.

She never looked up. She who boldly stared anyone in the eyes didn't look up.

What had he done?

More importantly…*why?*

So much wasted time and why? Because she had opened him up. Because she had seen him and it scared him. Submitting to her was the easy part. This entire audience was submitting to her without realizing it.

Loving Jessa was easy.

Luke had been doing it his entire life. What was so hard in that? It was impossible for him to imagine submitting to anyone else but Jessa. Fuck, he couldn't even contemplate loving anyone else but her. Her voice wove through his thoughts, dragging him into this arena filled with thousands of people who didn't know her. Even her parents didn't know her completely. They didn't know there was a sadistic streak within her that enjoyed torturing him with pleasure.

"I'm lost and alone without you. It's coldness and darkness when I can't touch you. Where are you hiding, my prairie blue?

Her voice held that last word until it sank deep into his soul. The two spotlights snapped off into darkness as she abruptly cut the note off. Pause-pause. A heartbeat in the darkness. One hand beat on a guitar and he knew it was hers.

"Everywhere I roam, I wonder."

There was total silence. He counted his own heartbeats. Five. He knew she wasn't on the stage anymore. Both she and Griff were gone as suddenly as the lights and her voice. The crowd erupted and all the lights came on. He stared at the empty stool where Jessa had been.

The metal chairs on the floor squeaked as people stood. "That was *awesome*," someone said behind him. "I love her."

Sitting there, he felt numb. Everyone in this building said that. *I love her. I love, Jessa Brody.* As Jessa had said, they loved the dream of her.

Who knew that as a kid she sat on the floor of the barn and sing to the animals? Who had seen her as a teenager sitting in the middle of the pasture arms wrapped around her knees while she rocked back and forth, crying because no one had known if her dad was going to live? Who had sat beside her that night?

"You make her vulnerable."

He blinked and looked away from the empty stool. Robin Mathers sat beside him, her blonde hair soft and shiny beneath the harsh lights. The faintest hint of a tear still clung to her cheek.

"She may yield the crop, Luke, but she also bleeds at the blow."

"I know," he said.

Robin stared at him. "Do you? We have the safe words," she said in a soft voice. "We know that when we utter those words the physical pain stops but that's within *that* relationship. This isn't about who's the Domme and who's the sub. This is real. This is the heart and there's no safe word allowed. You make her strong and that means you make her vulnerable. *You*, Luke. No one else. Just you." Robin stood up and walked toward where the others stood, their access to the backstage in their possession.

He looked back at the stage. The stool was gone.
Like Jessa.

The hot ache within threatened to devour him. *Jessa.*

Clasping his hands behind his neck, he looked at the floor unable to stare at that empty spot anymore.

Sitting on the tailgate of a Brody Ranch truck, Jessa stared at the shadowy ground. A hole was there, waiting. Waiting to be filled, waiting for a foundation to be laid. Her house would go there and then it would be a hole no more. It was nice to know some pits could be filled.

The one gaping within her was another thing entirely.

The concert had been a success. There was no other word to describe it. Jessa wished she had retained a lot of it. It had been a hazy, empty blur. For the entire time, she had been highly aware of Luke sitting between his mother and Robin.

"So this is your hole."

She peeked at the man lounging beside her. He looked bad-ass in his beat up leather jacket and black jeans. The man even wore worn out biker boots. One didn't look at Mason Griffon and immediately think he played country music. Everything from his clothing to the intricate tattoo of a skull that had a whip slithering through the eye sockets instead of a snake screamed hard metal. His attitude was "don't fuck with me or you will bleed." One ballsy reporter had called him the bad boy of country. The interviewer had bitten off more than she could chew when he had looked at her with his almost black eyes and said, "Honey, there's nothing boy about me." The woman had stammered.

"Bet it looks nicer in the sunlight." He squinted up at the stars then at her. "As opposed to one in the morning. When normal people are *not* out staring at a huge pit. Why are we here, Jess?"

She hadn't wanted to stay at the ranch after the show. She felt drawn and quartered. That had been the longest show of her life with the new song looming over her head. The rest of the boys had thought she had been crazy to perform a song that was shiny and new and not on the new album. "It'll be everywhere," Halo had groaned.

Surprisingly it had been Griff who had said they'd do it. With him behind her, the others had reluctantly agreed.

A hand smoothed along her head and she rested it on his shoulder, taking the comfort he offered. She liked that with Griff there was no "I told you so."

"What do I do, Griff?"

"Tough girl." He kissed the crown of her head. "You'll be okay."

Would she? It didn't feel that way.

"Robin invited me to stay with her for awhile." It was tempting. The O'Connors wouldn't be here long. There were two more days of the Stampede, followed by her final concert for the rodeo participants and then her parents' post-Stampede bonfire and barbecue. It had become a Brody-O'Connor tradition that she missed for a long time because she was usually touring or recording.

Then Luke would return home.

"Coward," Griff said softly. "Haven't you hidden from him long enough? I've seen you make a grown man cry and beg, Jess. You torment a man, you don't hide from him."

"He's not like the others. They were…" She searched for the right word.

"Practice. I know. He matters. He always has. Are you sure I can't beat him up? Give me five minutes with your sub and I could make him a slobbery, bawling pile of goo on the floor while making him beg for more."

Griff could. He had before.

"You're sweet, Mason." Kissing his cheek, she fell quiet.

The faint rumble of a diesel engine drifted through the night. It grew closer and she shifted her gaze to watch a pair of headlights. Her heart gave a little kick when the pick-up pulled up beside them. From the light reflecting off the side of their own truck, she saw Luke in the driver's seat.

"Begging, Jess," Griff said in a low voice, anticipation at following through on his promise rich in his voice.

Luke left the truck running as he climbed out. The gravel road crunched beneath his feet as he walked toward them. He looked tired. Good, but tired. He stopped and she wished he hadn't come.

"Five minutes," Griff continued. His arm slipped away and he sprang down from his seat like a sleek, elegant panther. Griff approached Luke. Even in the faint light, she saw the wariness in Luke's eyes. A shoulder rolled as the two men came face to face. "Begging," he repeated in a low tone.

It was tempting really tempting to watch Griff unleash himself. He prowled around Luke who shot her a nervous look.

"Or," her friend continued, "I could just beat the shit out of him then kick his sorry ass back home to Mama."

"You could try," Luke said, poking the bear with a toothpick. "Can I talk to you?"

Her shoulder lifted in a shrug. "Talk."

"I'm sorry, Jessa."

Behind Luke, Griff moved. His foot pressed against Luke's knee. "You beg on your knees, cowboy."

It was as if his knees had become hinges. One minute Luke was standing and the next he was kneeling on the ground.

"Oh, I can see why you like him." Griff braced his hands on his thighs as he squatted. "He's very obedient. For the most part." He spoke to Luke then, a low murmur she couldn't hear from where she sat.

Griff straightened and walked to Luke's truck.

"Wait. Can I have the bag in the back?"

Curious, Jessa watched Griff reach into the truck's back and drag out a duffle bag. He flung it toward Luke then eased into the driver's seat. The door made a loud bang in the night. As she sat there while Luke kneeled, Griff backed up then drove away, leaving them in the night.

One of her legs swung as it dangled over the gate. Deep within that ache began to ease. Silly. Never had she thought she'd be one of those women who would get all melty with two stupid words and no explanation.

"I realized something tonight," Luke began.

"No." Leaning back on her hands, she stared up at the sky. "I don't want to hear you right now. Stay there." Sliding off her perch, she wandered toward her hole.

Was she willing to do this again? How many times were they going to do this? Squatting down, she picked up a rock from the road and rolled it between her palms. Wasn't there some kind of wise quote about repeating the same mistakes over and over again?

"Damn it." She tossed the stone into her pit and wandered over to Luke. He knelt on the gravel road, hands resting on his thighs while he looked up at the sky. The rocks crunched and rolled under her feet as she walked over to him. "Tell me what you realized."

If only there was more light to see him. The moon and stars only provided so much of a glow.

"I've spent the better part of my life wanting you, Jess, and that's not going to go away."

Crouching down, she met his gaze. Wanting was easy. She deserved more. "That's your big realization? That's you're a-ha moment?" Something he had already known. Maybe she should have let Griff Dom out on him because this was bullshit. "Wanting me is easy, Luke."

"I know. Anyone can want you. Everyone does. And anyone and everyone can say they love you."

Her breath caught in her throat and something that felt an awful lot like hope began to build. Okay, this was better than an "I'm sorry." Much, much better.

He didn't look away from her and she really wished she could see all of him for this moment. "But they just love a little piece of you. I, on the other hand, love *all* the pieces of you."

"Until when? The next time I do something that freaks you out?"

"Until forever, Jessa," he replied, his voice low. "So,

unhalt this, because I am not going anywhere. Do you want me to stay like this until dawn? I will. Just—" He swallowed and his voice broke a little "Unhalt this. Please, Mistress, unhalt this."

Unable to have even the foot of distance between them, she straddled him, settling on his lap. Her hand fisted in his hair and she tugged his head back. "Unhalt," she whispered before she kissed him, claiming his mouth. A low grunt came from him even as he gripped the back of her jean jacket.

"Rock."

"Good. Feel the pain, Lucas. Feel the pain." She slid her weight down more to his knees and swallowed his groan of pain with her mouth, drinking it down. He tugged on her jacket, striping it off before he grabbed her hips and pulled her up. Against her groin she felt the press of his arousal as their tongues claimed.

"This is too easy," she said as she caressed his cheek.

"What?"

"You should suffer."

He swallowed. "How so?" He caressed her ass and up her back. "Would you tie me up? Beat me until I begged for forgiveness?"

"Yes. Yes, I would." A shaky breath came from him at her answer.

"Bag," he whispered.

"What about it?"

"You left it in my truck from last Friday."

Had it really been a week since that horrible moment? Who was she kidding? Of course it had been a week. She had felt every one of those days, every hour, passing by painfully in her heart.

Really now. She looked toward the bag then at him. "You must think I'm pretty easy."

"Hopeful. I was hopeful."

"Did you peek?" His hands tightened at her question and she knew he had looked in the bag. "Bad boy." She stroked his cheek. "To see all my surprises for you."

"Just the rope. Saw the rope as I shoved some stuff in."

Stuff? Intriguing. "Stay." Climbing off him, she went to investigate what he had added. Crouching down, Jessa unzipped the bag and pulled out a camping mattress. Clever man. There were also some camping lanterns. "Hopeful, hmm? Looks like you were expecting me to swoon into your arms."

"Hopeful, Jessa. *Really, really* hopeful."

Picking up the sleeping pad, she threw it at him. He caught it but still didn't rise. "Unroll it in the back of the truck." The battery-operated lantern provided her some light and she swung it as she walked to the truck. Setting the lamp on the gate, she lit up the other two lights while Luke scrambled to his feet and jogged toward her, slipping on some of the rocks. Within minutes she was admiring the way he squatted as he unrolled the thin pad. "Take off your shirt."

He glanced at her and she withdrew one of the coils of rope. His gaze fell to the rope. The smooth hemp ran through her hand while she sat on the side of the truck. "Shirt. Off. Don't make me repeat myself."

"Yes, ma'am." Luke grinned then yanked his shirt over his head, tossing it at her.

She worked at the rope until she freed the end. "Do you know what I like about trucks?" She flicked the cleat that was used for tying things down in the truck—furniture, hay, Luke. "They're so bondage friendly." After making bowline knot she tossed the coiled rope onto the mattress. "Boots off."

"Not naked?"

"Why would I let you do what I want to do? Boots off, lie down." The other three ropes were tossed to where Luke was lying on the narrow pad. The light cast interesting shadows over his body and she wanted to trace and explore each darkened groove.

Jessa straddled him then sat down on his stomach. "I love bondage," she said as she made a single knot then laid it on the inside of his wrist. "There's a beauty in seeing a strong male bound and waiting for me." The end was wrapped under his arm then brought it up through the loop. She did this five times, making a bronze cuff on his arm.

The night was broken by his ragged breathing, his gaze bouncing from her to the rope then back again. When she tightened it, a low moaned grunt came from him and he arched up in an automatic response while she made a quick knot, effectively binding him to the truck. "Lovely," she whispered, her hands stroking down the rope and along his velvety skin. "Good?"

"Yes," he hissed. "God, yes."

Reaching behind her, she cupped his swollen cock and was rewarded with another grunt of pleasure as he arched, lifting her up. His fingers clutched the taut rope, holding it like a lifeline. His index finger stroked the hemp as if he were amazed that he was finally tied up. She grabbed a second rope, and repeated the process on his other arm.

There was something so earthly erotic about seeing a strong wrist bound. She stood and went to tie off the other end to the cleat close to the cab of the truck. The first rope wasn't taut enough so she tightened it, dragging another sexy sound from him.

Both of his hands were now clinging to the rope, feeling it not just against his wrists but also within his fingers. Luke was magnificent bound like that. "Describe it to me."

"Right," he breathed the word out. "It feels right."

It looked right. She knelt between his legs. His chest rose and fell with each hard breath he took. Her hands were less than steady as she opened the fly of his jeans then eased the denim over his erection. If him being tied up felt right, it was beyond right for her to be tying him up.

"Jessa." He sounded worried.

"Don't worry, cowboy, I won't let you come." On her knees, she backed up, dragging the jeans down his legs. She loved his legs. The muscles were so thick from a lifetime of being the only thing aside from his determination that kept him on a bucking horse. The dark hairs tickled her fingers while distinct lines appeared as he tightened his thighs.

When she peeked up, he was gripping the rope so hard his biceps were bunched. Her cowboy was thick with arousal, the head of his cock was visible at the waistband of his shorts. Resisting that naked flesh was difficult but necessary. That one touch could be what set him off. And that wouldn't do at all.

To prolong his torture, she neatly folded the jeans, smoothing the empty legs.

"Jess," he moaned. "Going to come. Really."

Smiling she set the jeans down then reached into the bag and found what was necessary for him not to come before she was good and ready to let him. There was the temptation to strip his shorts off to see how far she could push him. One leg bent and he braced his foot on the bed of the truck, as if that would ease him. Silly man.

"Breathe for me," she ordered as she drew the tight boxer briefs to mid-thigh. He didn't breathe. Luke panted while a sheen of sweat began to glisten on all that bared skin. His fingers were rhythmically squeezing the rope, strangling it. She flipped open the leather cock ring as she dropped to her knees. The thick base was cinched quickly and without teasing.

That athletic body bowed as a load moan ripped from deep within him. "Breathe." She caressed his taut stomach, the muscles rock-hard beneath his damp skin. Precum glistened in the lanterns' glow and she leaned down to capture the silky saltiness on her tongue.

"God, oh God," he moaned. "Stop, stop, stop, stop, stop." Since his plea wasn't halt, she ignored him, teasing the plump crown with her tongue. His hips pushed up, trying to shove his cock into her mouth.

"Do you want to come now?"

"Yes," he hissed.

"Without me finishing this? I have two more ropes and so much more in my bag, Lucas. What do you want?"

"Finish. Oh God, finish."

She loved accommodating subs. They were so…accommodating. She pressed a light, teasing kiss on his cock then removed his shorts. His legs were tied up like his arms until she had all six naked feet of Luke bound in the back of the truck.

Jessa reached into the bag, searching for the one thing she wanted. She set the spur beside his hip then sat down to remove her boots, setting them beside his. With her jacket somewhere in the dark, she had one less thing to remove. As she stripped off her shirt and bra, she folded them, not because she was a neat freak but for several reasons.

It prolonged the moment so Luke suffered just a little bit more but it also provided a break for his body already heightened from the rope. She wiggled out of her jeans and decided to leave on her panties.

"God, you're sexy," he whispered.

Through the fall of her hair, she looked at him as he watched, his head lifted. "Thank you. So are you. I like you like this. I may keep you like this forever." She traced the rope at one ankle.

"Oh please. Yes, please." His head fell down as if the muscle melted from his neck.

She caressed up the lines of his legs, luxuriating in the strength that was hers to control, hers to command, hers to hurt. There were no subs before Luke. They were ghosts now, pale in comparison to this man.

It was such a cliché thought but so true.

"I've wanted to do this for years," she whispered as she reached down beside him and picked up the spur.

Her nail flicked the rowel and enjoyed the metallic sound it made as it spun.

She rolled the cool metal over his stomach and up to his chest. The blunt yet smooth prongs pressed into his skin. Luke sucked in his breath and she loved the way his skin dented beneath each point not sharp enough to break flesh. Her hand tightened on the U-shaped yoke. "It was my first fantasy. You like this. Me like this." Kneeling between his legs once more she drew the spur down the path from his neck to his groin.

Jessa began to hum *Tempt Me* as she traced his body with the spur. He moaned her name, his body once more arching up. Down his thigh to his knee then up the inside of his leg. She knew how it felt. How it felt to have metal glide over the body, how certain spots sent flares of heat. She had lain in her bed with the spur, testing it out to see how hard she could press before it became pain and where that pain felt the best.

"Fuck. Mistress." Down the inside of his other leg, up his thigh, over his abdomen. Her own heart raced and she was as breathless as he looked. Her panties were soaked.

"You're so wet for me, baby." Her finger ran over the tip of his cock and she sucked the pre-cum off. "Me, too." Her hand slipped under her yellow lace bikini panties and she shivered when she found her wet pussy, weeping with need for him. The head of his penis was painted with her moisture then she rolled the spur along the underside of his cock.

"Fuck!" He yanked on the ropes. Over his balls she drew the rowel and he arched hard. "Jessa!"

She traced the thick vein on the underside of his cock

and she knew it was time to put down the spur by the way his entire body snapped taut. Jessa stripped off her panties, tossing them aside without looking to see where they landed.

"Fuck, Jess. Coming. Fuck me, Mistress. Fuck me. *Please.*"

She settled on him and he bucked at the wet press of her pussy. Jesus. God. His body was hot beneath hers and slick from sweat. The spur rolled over one breast and cream spilled from her.

"It *is* nice." Silver rolled along her other breast, over her nipple and down her stomach. Setting the spur down carefully beside him she enjoyed the way he writhed beneath her.

She leaned down to kiss him. Hot pants of air came from him as their tongues met, tasted and absorbed the other.

"Please. Want to be inside you. Need to be inside you. Jessa."

"Tell me again," she ordered in a whisper.

His lashes lifted and she was gazing into his prairie blue eyes. Arousal and heat burned in the color that was uniquely his but more than that there was his heart. "I love you, Jessa Mae Brody, but will you please just. Fuck. Me. Now."

"Never let it be said I never accommodated my sub." Shifting on him, her fingers stroked down his cock and she enjoyed the heat of his skin, the full hardness. When she reached the base where the leather cinched him, she glanced up. "You good?"

Luke took a deep breath then gripped the ropes hard.

Every muscle in his thighs contracted as he gave a jerky nod. She snapped open the cock ring then flung it aside. "Hate those," he growled.

"Cock rings?" She made a mental note to invest in some more if he hated them so much.

"Yes. In you. Now."

"You don't give the orders here." His chest received a sharp slap, rising on her knees she gazed down at him. He was beautiful. He was sexy. He was sweet. He was strong. He was Luke and he was hers. Hand gripping his cock, she slowly sank down onto him.

"Lucas?" His lashes lifted at his name and she leaned down to kiss him, her hips beginning a rhythmic roll. He sighed at the sensation. "I love you, too," she whispered. "Come."

That low, throaty sound he made escaped from him and he thrust up, his athleticism allowing him to plunge into her despite being tied up. Bracing her hands beside his head, one hard thrust sent him over the edge.

"Come, come, come," he whispered. "Come for me, Mistress."

Her own orgasm swept through her and she cried out his name as she rode him through it all before she sank onto him.

"Jessa Brody loves me," he said, a little bit of wonder in his voice.

Smiling against his neck, she reached up and fumbled with the simple knot at his wrist. "Yes she does." The rope gave way and a strong arm wrapped around her waist.

Jessa pulled away only long enough to free his legs. Curling against him, she reveled in the feel of him against her. "Jessa Brody wants to fuck my ass." This time there were nerves in his voice as she released his other arm.

She laughed at the words. "Yes, she does."

Luke caressed down her back then up until his fingers combed through her hair. "Yee-haw." Grinning at her laughter he rolled on top of her and swallowed the sound. "I'm ready for round two."

Chapter Ten

JESSA SHUT HER eyes as the crowd shouted. It was the last day of the Stampede and this was Luke's last ride. Their two families plus Robin and the band were sitting in the Grandstand's infield seats, a section of seating which put them up close and personal with the rodeo and the action. "Close enough to smell that bull's fart," according to Griff.

She was going to throw up. She was seriously going to throw up. She was going to grab Griff's tub of popcorn and throw up.

"You're missing the show, Jess," her friend said beside her.

God. Jessa couldn't look.

"Luke O'Connor," the announcer finished and her eyes snapped open. The chute opened and the bronc erupted, trying to shake the burr from his back. Grabbing Griff's thigh, she watched the sheer male beauty of Luke on the horse who was pissed he hadn't gotten rid of the cowboy. The horse leapt, twisted and kicked clods of dirt behind him. She couldn't look at the clock. She didn't dare.

Oh fuck, had it been an hour?

Sweet god, he was breath-taking.

Behind her she heard his mom screaming, but god, there was only Luke battling the horse. Dena O'Connor knew how to scream.

Jessa was pretty sure she heard her screaming at last night's concert.

Robin grabbed her forearm and Jessa damn near jumped out of her skin. Their friends and family had converged on the Stampede grounds, invading the Grandstand where the rodeo was every year. After the concert in the Round-up Centre, they were all heading back to her parents' ranch for a bonfire to unwind from the past ten days. Then while their parents visited, she was going to tie Luke up in the barn—though he didn't know that part.

"Rob?"

"Eye on the prize, Jess." Robin shifted her grip, grabbing Jessa's hand. Thank god, because she so needed to hold onto someone. She squeezed her best friend's hand hard.

"He's a prize, isn't he? He's so beautiful." So fluid as he held onto the handhold with one hand, the other above him, counteracting the bronc's movements. Did she hear a horn? She had no idea because Dena O'Connor was screaming while he was helped off the bronc and onto another horse. He immediately slid down and punched his fists into the air. She heard his shout over the crowd— clearly he got his lungs from Dena.

And, oh, how Jessa knew that.

Luke pointed at her and she pointed back. A fist

pounded his heart. She tapped her wrists together. Even from here she saw the shudder move through his body. She smiled slowly.

A ride like that deserved rope *and* spurs.

The End

Acknowledgements

Jessa and Luke's story has had an amazing journey and a lot of people helped them travel from idea to here. I wrote this story as a bit of a dare to myself. Could I write a female domme character? And more importantly would anyone want to publish it or read it? The answer to all the above was yes. This story was first published as Spurred On and I had an incredible editing team behind me. The book then transitioned to Domme for Cowboy when it became a part of the Stampede Sizzlers series: a series of steamy romances set during the Calgary Stampede. From there it branched out on its own. From the first publisher, Wild Rose Press, to it's current indie life, a lot of amazing people have been behind this book - too many to mention in this small space but please know I'm incredibly thankful. Thank you for supporting an unconventional heroine and the hero who loves her. Without your belief in either of them, this book would not exist.

Jenna

Bio

Jenna's writing dreams truly began one summer on the air mattress of her childhood home. There she tackled her first romance: a truly wretched attempt at a medieval historical. Upon finishing the purple prose laden story of (in her own words) crap, Jenna decided that perhaps the historical genre wasn't for her and she promptly began to write in a contemporary setting. If only the journey had been easy. She tackled category romances (and in her own words) felt like they were crap. She didn't have the patience for romantic suspense. Really, she just wanted to get to writing the sex. (hint hint, Jenna) Her romantic comedies were so traumatic that she stopped writing until one day she got a phone call from a friend who said "We can totally write this." The genre was erotic romance and it was (in her own words) like coming home. Residing in Calgary, Alberta, Jenna happily writes the naughty romances that make her mother sooooo comfortable. (not)

www.jennahoward.com